"I need your answer now."

Seth's voice was cold, almost contemptuous.

"Thank you for asking me," Kristin said, "but I can't accept the assignment."

A cool smile flicked across his face. "Because?" he said in a soft, ominous voice.

Kristin forced herself to smile politely and meet his gaze head-on. "Because," she said calmly, "I have commitments."

His mouth narrowed. "I thought you had no commitments."

She felt her cheeks grow warm. "I didn't say that exactly. What I said was—"

A look of distaste swept across his face. "Please," he said, striding past her to his desk. "Don't bother. The way you live is none of my business."

Kristin drew herself up. "No," she said, rigid with self-control, "it most certainly is not."

SANDRA MARTON says she has always believed in the magic of storytelling and the joy of living happily ever after with that special someone. She wrote her first romance story when she was nine and fell madly in love at the age of sixteen with the man she would eventually marry. Today, after raising two sons and an assortment of four-legged creatures, Sandra and her husband live in a house on a hilltop in a quiet corner of Connecticut.

Watch for Seth and Kristin, the hero and heroine of *By Dreams Betrayed*, to return in Harlequin Presents #1457, *Lost in a Dream*. They can't resist helping Seth's sister, Jeanne, find her "Mr. Right."

Books by Sandra Marton

HARLEQUIN PRESENTS
1244—EYE OF THE STORM
1277—FLY LIKE AN EAGLE
1308—FROM THIS DAY FORWARD
1347—NIGHT FIRES
1379—CONSENTING ADULTS
1411—GARDEN OF EDEN

Don't miss any of our special offers. Write to us at the following address for information on our newest releases.

Harlequin Reader Service
P.O. Box 1397, Buffalo, NY 14240
Canadian address: P.O. Box 603,
Fort Erie, Ont. L2A 5X3

SANDRA MARTON

by dreams betrayed

Harlequin Books

TORONTO • NEW YORK • LONDON
AMSTERDAM • PARIS • SYDNEY • HAMBURG
STOCKHOLM • ATHENS • TOKYO • MILAN

Harlequin Presents first edition March 1992
ISBN 0-373-11443-5

Original hardcover edition published in 1990
by Mills & Boon Limited

BY DREAMS BETRAYED

CHAPTER ONE

KRISTIN knew that she was dreaming. It was the sort of half-dream that came just before the icy plunge of awakening, when your mind told you that you were caught in a fantasy world and all you had to do to leave it was wake up.

Come on, Kristin, a little voice inside her was whispering. None of this is real. Open your eyes and wake up.

The dream was never exactly the same. Sometimes she was deep within a forest, the smell of pine sharp in her nostrils, or walking on the sun-warmed stones of a pebbled beach beside an aqua sea. But there was always a sense of anticipation, of waiting—and then, suddenly, her heart would begin to race, her blood to thicken.

This time she found herself in a meadow filled with wild flowers. Kristin paused and looked around her. Her breath caught. *Yes*. He was here, she could feel his presence. He was somewhere just ahead, waiting for her.

Wake up, Kristin, the voice within her urged. Come on—wake up!

She tried, but her eyelids were far too heavy. The dark sweep of lashes that lay against her cheeks trembled with effort, then stilled. With a soft sigh, Kristin fell willingly into the spiralling darkness.

The dream welcomed her like an old friend.

'Hello, Kristin.'

Beneath her thin silk nightgown, Kristin's breasts rose and fell with quickened speed. There he was, rising to his feet in the tall grass of the meadow. Mist swirled around him, obscuring his face. Still, she knew him: his husky voice, his broad shoulders, even the elusive scent of his cologne.

Kristin smiled. 'You're here,' she said in a whisper.

'Did you think I wouldn't be?'

'I—I wasn't sure.' She fell silent. 'Were you waiting for me?'

She thought he smiled. 'I've always waited for you.'

'Won't you tell me who you are?' she asked.

He laughed softly. 'You know who I am.'

'I don't,' she insisted. 'I've never seen your face. You won't let me.'

His voice roughened. 'You've never looked.'

'I have. But you always stand in the shadows.'

'And you never come close enough to see me.'

Kristin shook her head. 'I don't know what you mean.'

Her voice faded to silence. He was walking towards her, slowly, his pace more even than her erratic heartbeat. She could see him emerging from the haze.

'Wait,' she said, taking a hurried step back. 'Don't—don't come to me. I—I don't want—I'm not...'

Her feet were rooted to the ground. She closed her eyes tightly before he reached her. His arms closed around her, and she began to tremble.

'Kristin.'

Her name was a whisper in the still air, carrying within it everything she had ever hoped for. He drew her closer. Her head fell against his chest; beneath her ear, his heart was racing as swiftly as hers.

'You smell of violets,' he said softly.

'No,' she said. 'This is wrong. I can't...'

His mouth was at her temple. She could feel the heat of his lips, the coolness of his breath. God, she was melting, she was turning to liquid fire.

'How can something we both want so badly be wrong?' he whispered.

Kristin felt her heart lift with joy. She had waited so long for this, for the warmth of his embrace, the touch of his mouth...

'*No*,' she said again, but even as she said it her face was lifting to his, her hands were sliding up his chest to his shoulders, her lips were parting...

'*Kristin.*'

'Kristin...'

'Kristin! For heaven's sake, didn't you hear the alarm?'

Kristin's eyes flew open. Disorientated, she stared blindly at the figure beside the bed.

'Where is he?' she said. 'He was just...'

Her room-mate raised an eyebrow. 'Where's who?' she demanded grumpily. 'That must have been some dream. You were thrashing around in here like a fish on a line, muttering to yourself...'

She'd had the dream again, Kristin thought, sitting up and threading her fingers into the thick, dark hair that tumbled below her shoulders. It had taken her by surprise. Days had passed since the last time, long enough so she'd begun to think—to hope—it was gone forever. And now, damn it, it had returned, starting and ending just as it always did, leaving her no nearer understanding what it meant than when it had first begun last spring.

No. That wasn't true. The dream hadn't ended as it always did. This time, the man had taken her in his arms, she'd felt the hard press of his body, the heat of his lips...

'...loud enough to wake the dead, for God's sake. How could you have slept through it, when it was enough to wake me in the next room?'

Kristin blinked and stared up at her room-mate. Susan's face was puffy from sleep and flushed with irritation.

'I'm sorry, Suze.'

'Well, you should be. I've got a three-day layover. I planned on sleeping in this morning.'

'I really am sorry,' Kristin said, pushing aside the blankets and swinging her feet to the floor. 'I guess I got to sleep too late last night.'

The other woman sighed. 'Forget it,' she said, her pretty face relaxing into a smile. 'Come to think of it, sweaters are on sale at Saks. If I get an early start, maybe I can snag myself a cashmere.'

'What time is it, anyway?' Kristin said as she slipped her feet into the pair of blue satin mules lined up neatly beside her bed. 'I have to be in early. There's a meeting at nine, and my boss...'

'Relax.' Susan collapsed on to the edge of the mattress just as Kristin got to her feet. 'The alarm only just went off—you have lots of time.' She propped the pillows behind her and leaned back. 'So Attila the Hun wants you in early, hmm? Seems to me you should be going in late, considering how much overtime you put in last night.'

Kristin's eyebrows rose. 'Two hours, that was all. And it couldn't be helped. He needed to get some notes together for today's meeting. It's important.'

'Attila *always* says it's important.'

Kristin laughed as she slipped into the pale pink silk robe that matched her nightgown.

'Things are busy just now.'

'Things have been busy ever since you went to work for Seth Richards. The bastard's worked your tail off this past year.'

'It's only been six months,' Kristin said patiently. She clipped her long black hair on top of her head and turned to Susan. 'OK if I hit the shower first?'

Susan smiled. 'Sure. Saks will just have to wait for me. Seriously, why don't you ask for a couple of days off? I can probably get you a freebie ride to the Bahamas—we could take a long weekend.'

Kristin shook her head. 'It sounds lovely. But——'

'But Attila needs you. Honestly, you let that man get away with murder.'

Kristin sighed. 'What do you tell your captain when the flight you're working is delayed two hours on the ground, hmm? I'll bet you don't say, "Sorry, I can't work such long hours, I'm leaving."'

Susan grinned. 'Wouldn't I just love to try it, though?'

'But you can't, any more than I can tell Mr Richards I can't take his letters or get his notes typed on time. Not if I want to keep my job—and you know I do. This promotion...'

Her flat-mate held up her hands. 'I know, I know, you're thrilled to be out of the steno pool, thrilled to be moving up the ladder——'

'Thrilled I can afford my half of the rent on these elegant digs,' Kristin said, laughing as she walked across the narrow room to the window and drew open the curtains. The room filled with sunlight, or what passed for sunlight in the narrow canyons of Manhattan. 'What's the weather report for today, do you know?'

'Sunny and cool, I think the man said.' Susan yawned and snuggled into the blankets. 'Maybe I'll hit Saks later—this afternoon, after the first assault wave has secured the beachhead.'

Kristin slid open her wardrobe and peered inside. 'I wonder if it's cool enough to wear my new suit?' she mused, taking out a hanger and looking thoughtfully at the grey wool garment hanging on it.

Susan laughed. 'Is that a new one? Honestly, what's the sense of spending money on new stuff when it looks just like the old stuff?'

'A suit's a suit, Susan. What else should it look like?'

'I don't know. Different, that's all. Why do they all have to have straight skirts, single-breasted jackets, notched lapels...'

Kristin shrugged. 'I like tailored clothes.'

'Really?' Susan's voice fairly purred. 'Then how do you explain the silk nighties and négligés?'

There was a moment's silence. 'Silk things are made well,' Kristin said finally. 'They're—they're an investment.'

'Not if you haven't got a man to show them off to.'

'I have lots of men,' Kristin said airily. 'In fact, I have a date with Paul tonight. He's taking me to dinner.'

'And then safely home.' Susan sighed dramatically. 'It's too bad Attila's such a bastard. That look I had at him the day I met you for lunch stays with me. The man's a slave-driver, but he's a hunk.'

'Join the queue,' Kristin said lightly. 'There's a long line of others who'd agree.'

'Don't tell me Attila has time for a social life?'

'He manages,' Kristin said drily. 'I place enough orders with to florist each month to pay off the National Debt.'

The other girl grinned. 'Well, you know what they say about all work and no play.' She watched as Kristin hung her suit carefully on the door. 'And what about you? Do you agree?'

'Do I agree with what?'

Susan shifted lazily in the bed. 'That your boss is a hunk.'

'I suppose,' Kristin said. Her eyes met her room-mate's, and she laughed. 'Don't look at me that way, Suze. I guess he's good-looking enough. It's just that I never think of him that way.'

'Well, I don't much blame you.' Susan yawned. 'Attila works you like a dog.'

'It's no harder than he works himself,' Kristin said as she took a softly tailored silk blouse from the wardrobe and draped it over the back of a chair.

'Well, then. ...?'

'Well, then, what?'

Susan snorted. 'Well, then, why aren't you at the head of the line? Seems to me you'd have an edge on the rest of them, working side by side with the guy.'

Kristin sighed. 'I told you, Suze. The man's my employer.'

'Hey, come on. I worked in an office before I started playing waitress-in-the-sky. I know all about love among the filing cabinets.'

Somehow, Kristin kept her tone light. 'So do I. That's why it's not a game I want to play.'

Her room-mate sighed. 'Well, I'm not the Puritan you are. Listen,' she said, her voice rising to follow Kristin as she left the room, 'if Attila ever makes a pass at you, give him a lecture on morality and then send him along to me. OK?'

Kristin laughed despite herself. 'Will do,' she called as she stepped into the bathroom and switched on the light.

Trust Susan to bring things back into perspective, she thought as she slipped off her robe and nightgown, stepped into the shower, and reached for her bar of violet-scented soap. Once burned, twice shy, that was her motto. Not that she was ever going to tell anybody that she had been scalded by 'love among the filing cabinets'. The memory of the quick, painful episode she'd survived five years ago was still too humiliating. Young, naïve, she'd been seduced by her handsome boss into believing he was in love with her, just as she was with him.

But it hadn't been true. She'd sensed his withdrawal after a while. She'd heard rumours that he was seeing someone else, and she'd confronted him. Vincent had denied it.

'Things aren't always what they seem,' he'd said, and she'd given in, kidding herself, until the day she'd come to work and found him packing his things.

He'd been transferred, he'd said, not meeting her eyes, and by the time she'd managed to trust her voice, he was gone and out of her life.

All of which meant that working for Seth Richards, who never saw her as anything but his efficient secretary, was very much to her liking. And Kristin suspected her own attitude towards office affairs was part of the reason she'd landed her job.

She could still remember the day she'd been called down to Personnel for an unexpected interview. The week hadn't gone well up to that point. She'd been sharing this flat with two other girls; Jane had one bedroom, Debbie the other, while Kristin slept on a pull-out sofa in the living-room. As luck would have it, Jane had decided to marry her long-time boyfriend and Debbie had announced it was time to go to France if she was to get anywhere with her modelling career at the same time.

Both girls had moved out within days of each other and Kristin had been frantic. She knew she had to find new room-mates or give up the flat. Worse still, a week of having the place to herself had left her aching to at least keep to only one other tenant.

Not that such a thing had seemed even remotely possible. The rent was moderate for Manhattan, which meant it was exorbitant by any sane person's standards. And then had come the summons to Personnel.

It was company policy that open secretarial positions were posted on the bulletin board in the stenography pool. Kristin checked them over weekly; she'd even applied for one or two. But when the head of Personnel asked if she was interested in becoming Seth Richards' executive secretary, she was puzzled. She'd heard rumours about his secretary leaving, but...

'This opening wasn't posted, was it?' she'd asked.

The head of Personnel had smiled wryly. 'No, it was not. It came up rather suddenly. You've been with us for some time, Miss Marshall. And you've excellent ratings.' Her eyes had met Kristin's. 'Do you know our Vice-President in charge of development?'

Kristin had looked up sharply, wondering if the woman was serious. Seth Richards was a man on his way to the top, but that wasn't why the girls in the pool talked about him. They went on endlessly about his good looks, his bachelor status, the beautiful women seen on his arm at various Harbrace-sponsored events. But Mrs Dowd's expression had been grim; there hadn't been even the hint of a smile on her face.

'Yes,' Kristin had said, 'I know him. Well, I don't really *know* him, of course, but...'

'He sets a high standard for himself and for those who work for him. Your supervisor has noted your efficiency and dedication, and she assures me an occasional hour or two of overtime won't distress you.'

'I believe in getting the job done, Mrs Dowd.'

'What if the job involved travel? Would that be a problem?'

Kristin had shaken her head. She knew that Harbrace had several branch offices throughout the country.

'Not at all,' she'd said.

'Mmm hmm.' The personnel director had looked at Kristin approvingly, noting her neat French knot, discreet jewellery, and her well-tailored suit. 'Were you acquainted with Mr Richards' former secretary, Miss Marshall?'

'Linda Simpson? Yes, of course. We worked in the stenographic pool together.'

The older woman's eyes had met hers. 'I would hope you would have a certain professionalism Miss Simpson lacked.'

Kristin had stared at the other woman. 'I'm afraid I don't follow you, Mrs Dowd.'

The woman's nostrils had flared delicately. 'Let me be blunt, Miss Marshall. Mr Richards is interested in the excellence of your secretarial skills, nothing more. Is that clear?'

For one terrible second, Kristin had wondered if the head of Personnel had found out what a fool she'd made of herself so long ago.

But the thought had fled as quickly as it had come. The woman was talking about Linda. Of course—the rumours about the girl were true, then. Linda had been promoted out of the secretarial pool only a few months before, almost swooning over the fact that she was to be secretary to Seth Richards.

'My God,' she'd whispered, 'I'm going to be with him every day. That gorgeous man. How will I ever keep my mind on my work?'

She hadn't, apparently. Kristin felt a passing regret for the girl, and then a sudden flush of hope. This was the chance she'd dreamed of since coming to New York— she'd be secretary to one man instead of several, she'd have a little cubby-hole office of her own, and, best of all, enough money to pay half the rent on her flat.

As she'd smiled coolly at the head of Personnel, Kristin had already been mentally composing the ad she would run for a room-mate.

'Linda was naïve,' she'd said bluntly. 'I'm not. My only interest in Mr Richards is in his capacity as my employer.'

The personnel director had positively beamed. 'The job's yours, my dear.'

And a terrific job it was, too, Kristin thought now as she turned off the shower and stepped from the bath. Her work was interesting and the pay was good. Seth Richards had turned out to be a pleasant, if somewhat impersonal, man.

Barefoot, she padded into the bedroom. Susan was fast asleep, and Kristin collected her clothing quietly. She dressed in the living-room, then hurried to the kitchen and filled the kettle. There wasn't time for freshly brewed coffee today. Her boss had an early meeting, and he had asked her to be at the office in time to arrange his notes.

Actually, she was almost always several minutes early. It was a practice she had begun the first day she'd reported to him for work. Kristin spooned a teaspoon of Nescafé into a mug, then filled it with boiling water, stirring the dark brew as she remembered that morning.

She'd been a little nervous as she knocked lightly at the half-closed door to her new boss's private office, then stepped inside. He had been standing at the window behind his desk, staring out at the city below.

'Excuse me,' she'd said politely, and he'd turned towards her.

It was the first time she'd seen him this close. There was no pretending he wasn't good-looking, she'd thought. It wasn't just his face—those hazel eyes flecked with gold, that long, straight nose, the high cheekbones and hard mouth. Nor was it just his height or the lean whip-hard body hinted at beneath the perfectly tailored suit. His looks went beyond the obvious; there was a presence about him, a kind of power that said he knew he was in charge. It wasn't vanity or conceit; it was, rather, an awareness, a sense of self that told the world Seth Richards could vanquish it, no matter what the odds.

For a second, Kristin had wondered if perhaps she'd judged her predecessor too harshly. Maybe he had been the one to come on to Linda. The rumour mill had it that he never mixed business with pleasure, but the rumour mill had been wrong before. And even here, at this somewhat conservative Wall Street firm, executives sometimes dallied with their secretaries. Not openly; nobody was that foolish.

But such things happened. They always had. She was living proof of that, wasn't she? She was...

'Miss Marshall?'

His eyes, as cool as his voice, had swept dispassionately over her, coming to rest at last on her face and she had felt the tension drain away from her. She had known, in that instant, that she was of no more interest to him than his telephone or his fax machine.

'I hope you don't mind getting straight to work,' he'd said. 'I've a letter that must go out immediately.'

'Of course,' she had answered, and from that moment on she had been the perfect secretary and Seth Richards the perfect employer. It was true that she sometimes worked long hours, but he worked as hard as she did—although, from the bits and pieces of his private life she'd glimpsed over the past months, he played hard, too.

Kristin grimaced as she rinsed out her coffee-cup. What she'd told Susan was an exaggeration. It wasn't exactly the National Debt, but he spent a small fortune each month on flowers. Long-stemmed roses, orchids, flowers as sophisticated as the names and faces of his women.

Kristin had seen a few of them. Sometimes his dates met him at the office in order to make an early cocktail party or charity function. A tall, willowy Althea or Candice or Georgina would materialise beside her desk, sleekly dressed and coiffed, bringing with her a drift of Joy or Opium.

But, no matter how beautiful, none ever lasted more than a few weeks. There was a new name on the horizon now, Kristin thought as she hurried into the bathroom. Jeanne something or other. Lester. Jeanne Lester. Yes, that was it. Smiling a little, Kristin took her make-up from the cabinet. The name was old-fashioned, but she had no doubt that the woman would turn out to be another tall, elegant beauty.

Her glance fell on her watch as she dabbed a brush into a tin of blusher. It was going on eight. She was going to have to hurry. Quickly, she dusted the brush lightly over her cheeks, then ran a pale pink lipstick over her mouth. It was the only make-up she wore—her lashes were dark and thick, and shadow tended to make her violet eyes look bruised.

It was her hair that took time and effort. Kristin made a face as she brushed it back from her temples with long, hard strokes. Her hair was very long, it fell halfway down her back, and it took forever to pin into its usual French twist. Sometimes her arms ached by the time she was done.

'You have such gorgeous hair, Kristin,' Susan was always saying. 'If mine looked like that, I'd never pin it up.'

Kristin sighed. But she would, if she worked at a firm as conservative as Harbrace. She pursed her lips as she gathered her hair and drew it away from her face. Maybe it was time to get it hacked off. After all, what was the point in keeping it long when she never wore it loose? Nobody ever saw it...

She stared into the mirror. *He* saw her hair loose, the man she dreamed about. She always wore her hair down when he came to her. He liked it that way; she knew he did. She could sense it. He liked everything about her— the silk gowns she wore, the heavy fall of her dark hair, the scent of violets on her skin...

The hairbrush fell from Kristin's hand and clattered into the basin. She blinked, then gave a shaky laugh. When you started to treat your dreams as reality, it was time to do something about them.

She stabbed the last few pins into her hair, then marched into the living-room and gathered her things together.

Susan was right. She *had* been working too hard. Ten and twelve hour days were beginning to take their toll; it was probably the reason she was having these silly dreams again. Yes, now that she thought about it, that must be why. She was exhausted. What she needed was a vacation.

What was it Susan had suggested? The Bahamas. Sun. Sand. Blue water. And a free round-trip ticket, to boot. Well, why not? She had the time coming to her, and she'd take it. Two days, anyway, a Monday and a Friday. And if her boss put up a fuss, she'd tell him—she'd tell him...

Kristin felt a surprisingly harsh jolt of irritation. She'd tell him that she was entitled to some relaxation, too, even if her idea of a good time wasn't quite the same as his.

Seth Richards would just have to get along without her for a little while.

CHAPTER TWO

KRISTIN left a note for Susan tacked to the bulletin board beside the refrigerator. 'Command Central,' they'd dubbed it, but, with two differing schedules, it was the only sure way of communicating.

'The Bahamas sound great,' Kristin wrote. 'How about next Friday? I'll call to confirm later this morning.'

The offices of Harbrace International were in lower Manhattan, supposedly a short trip by bus or train. But traffic usually turned the bus trip into a half-hour adventure, and the subway was always jammed. Kristin glanced at her watch as she stepped out of her apartment building and into the street. There was plenty of time. The bus, then. It would be crowded, but it was still a more pleasant way to start the day. As for the extra time the trip would take—that would give her the time to plan her approach to Seth Richards.

He would grant the request, of course. After all, she had lots of vacation time coming to her. But she had the feeling he wouldn't be pleased. Kristin grimaced as the bus reached her stop and she fought her way through the crowded aisle to the door. After all, a good machine never asked for anything, and his was about to.

When she reached her desk, the door to his office was closed. The light was glowing on her telephone: he was in already, she thought as she put her things away and set up her desk. Well, that wasn't too surprising; he had a meeting scheduled for nine. She glanced at the little clock on her desk. It was almost that now. She'd talk to him about taking the two days off as soon as his meeting ended. With luck, she could get things squared away before Susan left on her shopping spree. She'd call and tell her to go ahead and make whatever plans she——

The door to his office opened abruptly. Kristin looked up from her desk and smiled pleasantly.

'Good morning,' she said. 'I was just going to ring you, Mr Richards. It's almost time for your——'

'You're late,' he said bluntly.

Her eyes widened in surprise. 'No, sir, I'm not. It's not yet nine, and——'

He waved his hand in dismissal. 'Are my notes ready?'

She blinked at his curt tone. He was always polite, unfailingly so. He had been, from the first.

'Miss Marshall? I asked if the notes——'

Kristin rose to her feet. 'Here they are, Mr Richards. I put the pages into this folder. I thought——'

He strode rapidly to her desk and snatched the folder from her outstretched hand.

'You're not to put any calls through while I'm in conference.'

Kristin looked at him. It was an unnecessary instruction. She already knew that was his procedure.

She nodded. 'Of course, sir.'

A muscle moved in his jaw. 'Unless...'

'Sir?'

'Unless it's Miss Lester. If she phones, I'll take the call.' Kristin tried to keep her face from reflecting her surprise. This was definitely *not* procedure. He had given her explicit instructions the very first day. She was never to interrupt his meetings with personal calls. Her boss kept his private life and his public one separated; there was never a blurring of the lines between the two. And yet here he was, telling her...

'Miss Marshall?' His voice was silken. 'Are you having difficulty understanding me this morning?'

She flushed. 'No, sir. I'll put Miss Lester through if she calls. I understand.'

His eyes met hers. 'I assure you,' he said coldly, 'you do not.'

Kristin's face paled. 'I'm sorry. I only meant...'

His mouth thinned, hardening until it was barely a slash across his tanned skin.

'"I understand, sir. I'm sorry, sir."' His tone was a cruel imitation of hers. 'You sound as if someone's programmed you.'

Two bright spots of crimson rose in Kristin's cheeks. 'I was simply being polite,' she said stiffly. 'I apologise if I offended you.'

The cool mask dropped from his face for a moment. Kristin caught her breath; beneath it, his expression was bleak. The quick smile he gave her did nothing to change it, but when he spoke again his tone was apologetic.

'Forgive me,' he said. 'I guess I'm feeling irritable this morning.'

'That's—that's all right, sir.' Their eyes met and she managed to smile in return. 'Shall I make some coffee?'

He nodded. 'Yes, that would be fine, Miss Marshall.' He hesitated, as if he was about to say something else, and then he turned away and walked back into his office.

The conference lasted half the morning. His meetings were always businesslike, but they were often punctuated by the sound of easy laughter. There were no such sounds this time, Kristin noticed. And, when the door to his office finally opened and the section heads filed out, a couple of their faces reflected the same bewilderment she had felt earlier.

This was hardly the day to tell him she wanted some time off. Kristin caught her bottom lip between her teeth. If only she could wait until tomorrow. But Susan had already telephoned twice, bubbling with excitement the first time and demanding an answer the second.

'I have to know for sure by lunchtime,' she'd insisted. 'I already spoke to Peg and Lucy about switching schedules, and a guy I know says he'll get us a cottage right on the beach for half the going rate. But I've got to call them all soon.'

'I don't think I can get an answer this morning,' Kristin had replied, keeping her voice to a whisper. 'It's not a good day to ask for time off, Suze. Tomorrow might be——'

Susan had snorted. 'Tomorrow might be too late. For goodness' sakes, you're not asking for the moon. Attila owes you two weeks. How can he turn you down if you ask for two days?'

'He can do whatever he wants, Susan. I'm telling you, he's——'

'I'll call back at noon. You'll have to give me a definite answer then.'

'Suze——'

'What are you going to do, wait for *him* to suggest you need a rest? Come on, Kristin. Stand up to the man. It's about time he faced the fact that you have needs, too.'

Now, watching the glum faces of her boss's subordinates as they filed past her, Kristin wished she had never left that note on the bulletin board. But her roommate was right, she was entitled to a measly two days off. And if the past six months were anything to judge by, if she waited for Seth Richards to suggest she take some vacation time, she might well wait forever.

'Miss Marshall?'

She looked up, startled by the sound of his voice. He was standing over her desk, looking down at her. Thank God, she thought, that cold hostility was gone from his face. He looked as he always did: a little removed, a little unapproachable—and very handsome. No, she thought suddenly, he really wasn't handsome. His features were too strong for that. And he wasn't gorgeous, as Linda had said. That was far too feminine a word to describe someone so blatantly masculine.

He certainly was the best-looking man she had ever known. There was no doubt about that. Seth Richards was—he was...

'The Allen file?'

Kristin blinked. 'I—I'm sorry,' she said. 'I'm afraid I missed that. Did you ask me something?'

He nodded. 'I want the Allen file. Bring it into my office, please. I'll need you to take notes as I go through it.'

She nodded, while her frazzled brain tried to make sense out of the spin of the thoughts that had just raced through her head. What was the matter with her this morning?

'Certainly,' she said. 'I'll be——'

'Have I had any calls?'

Was he asking about Jeanne Lester? Yes, he must be. She hadn't phoned, and he was upset. He was...

'Miss Marshall?'

Kristin swallowed. 'No,' she said. 'No calls.'

He nodded. 'All right,' he said after a minute, 'get the file, please.' His eyes met hers, and his eyebrows rose. 'Is there something you wanted to say, Miss Marshall?'

Yes, she thought suddenly, I want to tell you that whatever's wrong will pass, that nothing's worth that dark look...

Her cheeks flushed. God! She really did need time off. She was—she was...

A little smile curved across his mouth. 'Well? What is it, Miss Marshall? Is my tie crooked or something?'

She swallowed again. 'Actually, I did want to...' Her eyes met his and, in her confusion the words she'd been trying to avoid tumbled from her mouth, 'I—er—I'd like to take two days off next week.'

His brows drew together. 'Two days off?'

She nodded. 'Yes. I—I thought I'd fly down to the Bahamas.'

He frowned and threaded his fingers into his hair. 'You might have given me a little more notice. There are some things on tap next week that——'

'I would have,' Kristin said quickly. 'But the chance only just came up. My friend suggested it this morning, and——'

Seth Richards' nostrils dilated. 'Your friend?'

Kristin nodded. 'Yes. We only thought of it this morning, you see, and——'

His face turned dark as a thundercloud. 'Well, I'm afraid you'll just have to tell your friend that it's out of the question. I can't spare you for the week.'

'I think you misunderstood me, Mr Richards. I haven't asked for a week, I——'

'I understood perfectly,' he snapped. 'You've decided to go off on a jaunt with no more warning to me than if you'd awakened with the flu and called in sick.'

Kristin bit down on her bottom lip. I've *never* called in sick, she wanted to say, not once in all these months. But instinct told her this wasn't the time to remind him of that.

'It's hardly a jaunt,' she said with all the polite assertion she could muster. 'It's just two days.'

His lip curled. '*Just* two days.'

She felt her spine grow rigid. She hadn't asked for a minute off in six months, despite the fact that the company owed her two weeks' unused vacation time; she hadn't taken any sick days and she'd never been so much as five minutes late. And, as if that weren't enough, she'd worked whatever overtime this man had asked—without complaint and without so much as a dime extra. Executive secretaries didn't qualify for overtime pay.

She had been all he'd asked for and more—and now, here she was, asking for nothing more than a long weekend, and he was acting as if she'd requested a month's leave.

And to think she had been feeling empathy for him only a few minutes ago. Kristin took a deep breath and raised her eyes to his. The uncompromising iciness she found there almost made her flinch, but she held her ground and met his stare head-on.

'Yes, sir,' she said, as if his sarcasm had passed her by, 'two days is all I'm asking. I'll see to it that my work's all up to date before I leave, of course.'

The gold flecks in his hazel eyes glittered dangerously. 'Will you, indeed?'

'Certainly.'

'But I'd assumed your work was always up to date, Miss Marshall. Are you telling me that it normally is not?'

His voice fairly purred with derision. Kristin's mouth fell open. She stared up at him and then, with effort, snapped her jaw shut.

'No, sir,' she said coldly. 'I am not telling you that at all. All I'm saying is that I won't leave anything undone. The girl who replaces me will——'

His teeth glinted in a cold smile. 'How simple you make it sound. What of your responsibilities, Miss Marshall? Don't they count for anything?'

Kristin gritted her teeth. It had been stupid to bring this up now. If only she'd waited. She should have gone into his office to make her proposal. Then, she'd be the one who was standing, he the one who was sitting. It was intimidating to have him towering over her this way.

'It *is* simple,' she said evenly. 'I'm trying my best to ensure that your routine won't be disrupted. That's why I'm only asking for two days off. And, as I've told you, with someone to take my place——'

'And, as I've told *you*, it's out of the question,' he said in a voice that shut off all further discussion. 'Now, if you'd get that file and your notepad, we'll get started.'

Colour rose into Kristin's cheeks as her boss turned on his heel and marched across the floor. She sat still for a moment, staring after his straight back, and then she reached for her pad and the Allen file and rose to her feet.

So much for all the politeness the man had shown her these past months, she thought—and double that for loyalty rewarded. A vision of herself stalking into his office and tossing the file, the notepad, and her resignation on his desk flashed before her eyes—and then she remembered her half of the rent on the apartment she shared with Susan and she puffed out her breath in defeat.

All right, she thought, smoothing back her hair with a trembling hand, all right, Mr Seth Richards, we have new ground rules now. There'd be no more easy compliance with his requests that she work late, no more missing lunch or bolting down a sandwich at her desk as she worked.

She had never turned him down, not even when it meant calling Paul or one of the other men she dated occasionally and cancelling her evening's plans.

Kristin's eyes narrowed. Well, that was about to change. The bastard would have to give her plenty of advance notice from now on. And there was no way he could complain to Personnel, either. No one, not even the great Seth Richards, was entitled to treat people as if they were slaves.

Chin raised, she strode to his office, knocked once, and entered. Even in her anger, the room had the same effect on her as it always did. She hesitated in the doorway, trying not to let herself feel daunted. The room was not unlike the man himself, she thought grimly: cool, spare, and impressive.

It occupied a large corner of the fortieth floor and took full advantage of the view of Manhattan spread below. Two walls were composed entirely of glass. One looked uptown, across a sea of roof-tops, the other out on the Hudson River, which stretched like a sluggish grey snake between the crowded waterfront streets of the city and the New Jersey docks. Wine-red leather chairs clustered around a low glass table to the left, mates to the low leather couch centred against the opposite wall. A series of signed lithographs stretched above the couch, leading the eye inexorably to the room's focal point, Seth Richards's massive walnut desk.

He was seated at it now, looking out at the river, his Moroccan leather swivel chair turned so that his back was to the door. Kristin's head tilted as she watched him. There was something in the line of his shoulders that seemed different, she thought. They were hunched, as if in defence—or, she suddenly thought, as if he were carrying a heavy weight.

For a second, she remembered the bleakness she'd seen in his eyes earlier that morning. He'd said he felt irritable. Perhaps it was more than that. If he were ill...

Why was she looking for excuses? *She* felt out of sorts lots of times, but she hadn't taken it out on anybody else. No, the man was just showing his true colours. Attila the Hun, she thought. Susan had been right all along. Squaring her shoulders, Kristin started towards him, her heels tapping lightly against the Italian tile floor.

She put the file on his desk, then took her usual place in the chair opposite. She crossed her legs, carefully drawing her skirt down over her knees, opened her notepad, and waited. After a moment, she cleared her throat.

He swung his chair around. 'Miss Marshall,' he said, and she nodded.

'Yes. I'm ready, Mr Richards.'

She looked down at her notepad, scratched the date in, and waited again. The seconds dragged on, and finally she lifted her head. He was staring past her, his elbows propped on his desk, fingers steepled under his chin.

Kristin cleared her throat again. 'Would you like me to come back later?'

He looked up, almost as if he was surprised to see her, and then he shook his head.

'No, no, I'd like you to get these letters done this morning, if you don't mind.'

How polite he was now, compared to the way he'd treated her just a little while ago. Well, he could afford to be polite, couldn't he? It didn't cost him anything. That was why he'd been so even-tempered and courteous all these months. She had never asked anything of him, or turned down his requests, or...

His chair squeaked as he pushed it back and got to his feet. 'Where were we, then, Miss Marshall?'

'You said you wanted to see the Allen file,' she said, frowning a little and nodding towards where the file lay on his desk. 'You said you had some notes to dictate.'

'Oh. Right, right.' He picked up the file, opened it, then closed it again. 'First, send a letter to Craig Allen, Allen Associates, et cetera, et cetera. Dear Craig, I've been reviewing our discussion of last week and...'

His voice tapered to silence. Kristin looked up, puzzled. He never paused during dictation. His thoughts flowed easily, from start to finish. It was one of the things she liked about taking his letters; unlike some of the men she'd dealt with when she was in the stenography pool he never went back and struck things out, nor did he ever need prompting.

But he did now. He was standing at the north window, his back to her, staring down at the street. She had never seen him like this before, and all at once the anger that had moments ago consumed her was gone.

'Mr Richards?' she said softly.

He turned towards her, frowning. 'Sorry. Where was I?'

Yes, she thought, something was definitely wrong. His eyes were shadowed; they seemed to look beyond her into a darkness only he could see.

Kristin swallowed, then looked at her notes. '"I've been reviewing our discussion of last week,"' she read, trying to keep any sign of bewilderment out of her voice.

He nodded. '...of last week. And I find that your capitalisation figures may—may...'

She looked up again. He was staring at her, and the expression on his face was disconcerting.

'Is—is something wrong?' she asked.

He shook his head. 'No. I mean...' He sighed. 'About your request for time off, Miss Marshall. I—I didn't mean to take your head off.'

She searched for something to say. But an apology was the last thing she'd expected. Still, when you weighed it against everything else that had happened this morning, it wasn't really so surprising. Nothing that had gone on so far had been ordinary.

Maybe he really wasn't feeling well. That would explain his behaviour—although he didn't look ill so much as he looked exhausted. Dark shadows lay under his eyes, and the faint lines that rimmed his mouth looked knife-etched.

Something undefined stirred deep within Kristin's heart.

'That's all right,' she said with a little smile. 'I shouldn't have dropped it on you that way. Without any warning, I mean. I didn't realise...'

He smiled back. 'I'm sure we can work something out. Perhaps you could take some time off in a week or so. Early next month, maybe.' His smile broadened. 'In fact, why don't you plan on the entire first week in——?'

Kristin shook her head. 'That's very kind of you. But I'll have to check. I'm not sure my friend can take the whole week.'

'Your friend.' His smile dimmed and grew as weary as the expression in his eyes. 'Yes, I forgot about him. Well, we certainly can't expect you to disappoint your young man, can we?'

'You don't understand,' she said quickly. 'It's not——'

He held up his hand. 'You're right,' he said curtly. 'I don't understand.' His smile grew fixed. 'But I've been told that before.' He tossed the file on his desk and turned to the window again. 'All right,' he said softly, 'go on and take your trip. I'm sure you're right, I'll manage to get along without you for a couple of days.'

Kristin waited for the sense of elation his words should have brought. Instead, she felt a curious flatness.

'Thank you,' she said slowly. 'But now that I think about it, I'm not sure I——'

The shrill ring of the telephone silenced her. She stood and reached for the receiver.

'Mr Richards' office.'

The voice at the other end was casual and softly feminine. 'Hi. This is Jeanne Lester. Is Seth in?'

'Just a minute, Miss Lester. I'll see if——'

He snatched the phone from her hand before she could finish the sentence.

'Jeanne?' The one word gave everything away. It was as filled with tension as his face.

Kristin was already moving quickly towards the door. Instinct told her this was a conversation that needed privacy. She could feel his eyes burning holes in her back and she quickened her steps until finally she stepped into the outer office and pulled the door shut after her, but not before she heard him speak again.

'I hope to hell you've come to your senses,' he growled. 'All that nonsense last night, questioning what we both know is best. You know what our relationship means to me, Jeanne. I can't believe that you'd...'

Kristin walked to her desk and sat down. Well, she thought, that explained everything. She felt a sudden tightness in her throat.

Seth Richards wanted Jeanne Lester, but she didn't want him. It was hard to believe, but that was the way it sounded. What else could all that had happened this morning mean?

The tightness in her throat expanded until it was an aching knot. What a foolish woman this Jeanne Lester must be, to question her relationship with a man like Seth Richards. No woman in her right mind would— would...

Kristin put her hand to her mouth. No, she thought with a sudden, lurching dizziness, it wasn't Jeanne who was the fool.

It was she.

CHAPTER THREE

KRISTIN held her breath as she unlocked the entrance door to her flat. It was late, which meant that with luck Susan would be tucked safely away in her own room. God, she hoped so. The last thing she wanted just now was...

Damn! The ghostly image of some ancient episode of *I Love Lucy* flickered on the TV screen. She could see her room-mate sprawled on the sofa, a bowl of popcorn balanced on her belly. She sighed and let the door swing shut.

Susan shifted the bowl to the table and swung her feet to the floor.

'Well,' she said cheerfully, 'you're finally home.' The television screen faded to black as she aimed the remote control at it, and then she glanced at the clock. 'Almost eleven,' she said with a smile. 'You must have had a good time. You're never out this late on a weekday evening.'

Kristin turned away and put her handbag on the small table near the door.

'I thought you'd be asleep by now,' she said.

Susan yawned and stretched lazily. 'I figured I'd wait up for you,' she said. 'Did you and Paul go to dinner at that new place I told you about?'

There was a barely perceptible pause, and then Kristin shook her head.

'No.'

'Well, it's just as well. You'd probably have stood in line forever. It's so silly that they don't take reser-

32

vations. I guess they just like seeing people queueing at the door.'

'How was the sweater sale?' Kristin asked over her shoulder as she headed down the hall to her room. 'Did you buy Saks out?'

Her friend laughed as she rose from the couch and padded after her.

'Would you believe I never got there? I was just stepping into a taxi when somebody called my name. It was Donna Ames—we went through flight attendant school together. We haven't seen each other in ages, and we ended up stopping for lunch and, well, the day just got away from me.' She drew her robe together and plopped down cross-legged in the centre of Kristin's bed. 'So, how was it?'

'How was what?'

Susan groaned. 'Your date with Paul, of course. Did you have fun?'

Kristin hesitated again, and then she shrugged her shoulders. 'I didn't see him,' she said as she slipped off her suit jacket and hung it carefully away. 'I had to cancel at the last minute.'

'Cancel?'

'Uh huh.' She kicked off her grey suede pumps, then stepped out of her skirt. 'Something came up at work. Mr Richards needed some reports done, and——'

Her room-mate's eyebrows rose. 'But you had a date. What did he say when you told him that?'

Kristin reached into her wardrobe. Her hand brushed against her silk robe as she reached past it to pull an old flannel robe from the wardrobe's depths. Somehow, she yearned for its warmth and comfort tonight.

'I didn't tell him,' she said as she slipped the robe on and tied the sash around her waist.

'You didn't...?'

'No. There wasn't any point. He got a last-minute call about an important meeting for tomorrow, and he needed some reports done to take with him.'

Her room-mate puffed out her breath. 'Well, Attila certainly outdid himself this time. Making you break a date, keeping you chained to the typewriter until this hour...'

'I didn't mind. I mean, it wasn't his fault.'

Susan snorted. 'I'll bet he didn't even ask you if you had plans for the evening.'

'But he did. He asked me...'

'Yeah? Well, a lot of good it did. You told him you had plans and he told you to cancel them. Isn't that right?'

Kristin blinked. 'Actually—actually, I didn't tell him about my dinner date with Paul.'

Susan stared at her. 'Didn't tell him? Why on earth not?'

The women looked at each other, and then Kristin's glance slid away from her friend's face.

'Because he needed me,' she said, sitting down at her dressing-table.

Susan laughed. 'He *always* needs you, that's the trouble.'

'Not the way he did tonight. He had a bad day. He...' Their eyes met in the mirror. Kristin flushed. 'Come on,' she said briskly, 'tell me about this girl you bumped into. Does she fly with United Airlines, too?'

Her room-mate sighed. 'Yes, but she's on international routes, the lucky so-and-so.'

Kristin smiled. 'That must be lovely,' she said, lifting her hands to the French twist at the back of her head. She pulled out the clips that held it fast, and her long, black hair tumbled to her shoulders, framing her pale face. 'So, how was your evening? Did you go out or——'

'I had a dinner date, and then I came home and took it easy—which is what you could have done if you hadn't let Richards get away with murder. Nobody has the right to keep his secretary until ten o'clock and expect her to——'

Kristin swung around and glared at her room-mate. 'Damn it,' she said in a tight voice, 'what is this? I appreciate your concern, but I'm not a child.'

Silence settled over the room, and then Susan rose to her feet.

'No,' she said coldly, 'you're not.' She turned quickly and marched to the door. 'Good night, Kristin.'

'Suze—Suze, wait. Please.' Kristin rose, too, and hurried after her. 'I didn't mean it that way.' She put her hand lightly on the other woman's shoulder. 'I guess I'm more tired than I realised,' she said, smiling a little. 'Forgive me, please.'

'I was only thinking of your welfare,' her room-mate said stiffly.

'I know that. Really, I'm sorry.' Her smile broadened. 'Tell you what—how does a cup of hot chocolate sound?'

Susan stared at her, and then she let out her breath. 'It sounds good,' she admitted, and she smiled in return. 'Especially if we have some chocolate-chip cookies with it.'

In the kitchen, Kristin measured out the cocoa and sugar while Susan poured milk into a pan, then peered into the cupboards.

'We're out of cookies,' she said mournfully.

Kristin smiled. 'Too bad. But I'm full, anyway.'

'Aha! Attila ordered dinner in, did he? I hope you had something substantial.' She slammed the last cupboard door closed. 'Roast beef or steak, at least.'

A smile curved across Kristin's lips. 'We had pizza,' she said softly.

'Pizza? For supper?'

'Yes. And it was wonder——'

'Look out, the milk's boiling over.' Susan reached past Kristin and snatched the pan from the burner. 'Go on, get the mugs,' she said with a laugh. 'You're too tired to be useful.'

The women sipped the hot drinks in companionable silence for a while, and then Susan clapped her hand to her forehead.

'I almost forgot to tell you. I got us on an early flight to the Bahamas next Friday morning. And the hotel's in the bag—a two-bedroom suite, if you please, right on the beach. I couldn't get it for free, exactly. But it's the next best thing—we'll pay for regular rooms, but we'll get the suite instead. There's a terrace and a sitting-room, and they'll treat us like visiting royalty.' She grinned. 'How's that sound?'

Kristin swallowed. 'Lovely. But——'

'We'll fly back to New York late Monday, unless you think you can talk your boss into giving you a couple of hours off Tuesday morning. There's a flight that would get you to the office by noon, and——'

'Suze, it sounds wonderful. But I can't.'

Susan sighed. 'No, I didn't think so. Well, that's OK. We'll have four wonderful days of sun and gorgeous men and . . .'

'Suze.' Kristin took a deep breath. 'I can't go with you.'

Her room-mate's mouth fell open. 'Can't go? But just this morning, you said——'

'I know. But things changed.' Kristin pushed her chair back from the table. 'I tried calling you in the afternoon. But there was no answer.'

'I told you, I met this old friend . . .' Susan stared at her. 'What happened?' she asked, and then she gritted her teeth. 'Never mind, it's a dumb question. That bastard you work for——'

'He's not a bastard,' Kristin said quickly.

'He is, if he won't give you a measly two days off. Honestly, I don't understand you. Why don't you stand up for your rights?'

'I'm sorry if I've messed things up for you, Suze. I mean, you've made all these arrangements...'

Susan waved her hand. 'Oh, that's no problem. I can cancel them with one phone-call. Or I can give somebody else a ring and invite them along. Donna—the girl I bumped into today—she might want to go. It's just that I hate seeing that man walk all over you.'

'It wasn't his fault.'

'How do you figure that? You asked for the time off, and Attila said——'

'He said I could have it.'

The women stared at each other. 'He said what?' Susan said after a moment.

Kristin flushed. 'He wasn't thrilled, but he said I could have the days, if I needed them.' Her eyes met her friend's and then slid away. 'But I—I could see it wasn't a good idea to take the time next week. Things are really very busy at work right now, and—and...'

'And you're crazy,' Susan said flatly.

Kristin shrugged her shoulders. There was no sense in arguing, not when the same thought had occurred to her earlier.

'Come on, Kristin, come with me. It's just two days.'

'I told you, I can't.'

Susan sighed. 'Well, I just hope all this dedication is worth it. You'd better get a big fat Christmas bonus cheque or I'll personally blacken your Mr Richards' eye.'

Kristin turned around and smiled. 'I'll remember that, come December.'

'You'd better remember it next weekend, too, when I'm toasting to a golden tan and you're shivering in an autumn chill.'

Kristin's smile broadened. 'Don't forget to send me a postcard.'

Her room-mate nodded grudgingly as she rose from the table. 'You tell your boss he's got a one-in-a-million employee,' she said, putting her empty mug in the sink. 'Goodnight, Kristin.'

Kristin nodded. 'Goodnight.'

As soon as Susan's footsteps had faded, Kristin sighed and leaned back in her chair. One in a million... What would Susan say if she knew Seth had used those very words only a couple of hours ago?

'You're one in a million, Miss Marshall,' he said, standing beside her desk, the finished reports in his hand. She looked up, flushing with pleasure, and he smiled. 'How did you ever get these done so quickly?'

'Thank the new typewriter, not me,' she said with an answering smile, and that was when he insisted on having supper sent in.

'No,' Kristin said at once. 'I mean, that's very kind. But it's not necessary.'

'But it is,' he said, frowning as he glanced at his Rolex. 'Do you have any idea what time it is, Miss Marshall?'

She hadn't. They'd been working straight through since late afternoon, just after he'd received word that he had to fly to the company's Boston branch for a meeting the following day. That call had displeased him, too—she had seen the sudden irritation in his eyes, heard it in his voice as he'd barked at whatever hapless associate was on the other end of the line.

'I know it's late,' she said. 'But it doesn't matter, Mr Richards. I can grab a bite when I get home.'

'Don't be silly. You'll probably want nothing so much as a hot bath and a soft bed by then. It will do us both good to order something in.' He looked down at her. 'Unless, of course, you have an appointment.'

Kristin had a sudden image of Paul, waiting for the phone call she'd said might come if she finished work before it got too late. He'd been disappointed when she broke their dinner date—the least she owed him was a call now, followed by a drink or late supper.

'No,' she heard herself say, 'I have no appointment.'

He smiled. 'That's settled, then.' He sat down on the edge of her desk, his hand brushing hers as he reached for the telephone directory. 'What would you like? Sandwiches from the place down the block?' His smile grew. 'How about pizza? I haven't had one in years.'

'Me, neither,' she said, smiling in return. 'That sounds great.'

But the local pizzeria didn't answer. 'I should have figured that,' Seth said, frowning as he thumbed through the directory. 'This is a commercial area—I'll bet nothing's open after six.'

Nothing was. After the fourth useless call, he slammed down the phone and glared at it.

'Damn! Well, it's my own fault. I should have thought of having supper sent in hours ago.'

Kristin pushed back her chair and stood up. 'That's all right,' she said quickly. 'I really should go home. It's late, and——'

'I was all set for that pizza,' he said.

She laughed. 'Me, too. But...'

He cocked his head to the side. 'Well, then,' he said slowly, 'I have the perfect solution. Do you like pepperoni pizza?'

'But you just phoned.'

'Or mushroom? Which?'

Kristin smiled. 'You're torturing me,' she said. 'I like both.'

'I know this great place in Little Italy. We can take a taxi and be there in no time.'

Her heart lurched. She felt a sense of exhilaration so fierce that it stunned her. When she thought she could speak without giving herself away, she shook her head.

'Thank you, but I can't.'

Seth Richards looked at her. 'Your face is like an open book, Miss Marshall.' His words were soft, but she could hear the teasing laughter in his voice. 'I assure you, this is all perfectly proper.'

Kristin felt herself turn scarlet. 'I didn't think it wasn't. But——'

'This isn't some smoky little café,' he said gently. 'I'm not going to try and compromise you.'

Her blush deepened. 'Mr Richards...'

He sighed and ran his fingers through his dark hair. A lock of it fell forward across his forehead, and suddenly he looked as she had never before seen him—younger, somehow, and totally disarming.

'Look,' he said, 'I'm just trying to make amends for working you so hard. What would Mrs Dowd think if you complained about me? "He works his secretaries ten hours a day," you'd say, "and he starves them, too. There are chain marks on my ankles".'

She thought of what Susan had said about her being chained to the typewriter, and she laughed softly. Still, she shook her head.

'It's the thought that counts, Mr Richards. It was nice of you to offer, but——'

'Is there such a difference between sharing a pizza here, in the office, or in a noisy restaurant?'

'Yes. I mean, no. I mean——'

Kristin broke off helplessly. What did she mean? she thought, looking into his smiling face. He would take her to some brightly lit pizzeria, a place about as romantic as a pharmacy, they'd eat and have coffee, and then they'd go their separate ways.

It was all so innocent. Then why was she hesitating? Was it that sudden jolt of excitement that had raced through her moments ago, when he'd first suggested taking her to dinner? Or was it the way she'd felt all day, as if she had suddenly seen Seth Richards as a human being—as if she had suddenly realised he was a man?

'Have some pity, Miss Marshall.' She looked up, startled, and found him watching her with laughter glinting in his eyes. 'I'm starving to death.'

For God's sake, she thought, I'm making an ass of myself. 'So am I,' she said briskly, and she got to her feet. 'Thank you, Mr Richards. I'd be happy to share a pizza.'

The place he took her was, as he'd promised, no smoky little café. But it wasn't the kind of shabby pizzeria she'd anticipated, either. Instead it was a tiny restaurant, the sort of place Kristin had thought existed only in films. Sausages and cheeses hung from the rafters, perfuming the air. There was sawdust underfoot, and the waiters wore starched white aprons that stretched almost to their ankles. And the food—the food was the sort about which restaurant critics wrote purple prose.

'Are you sure you want pizza?' Seth asked after the menus had been handed to them.

She wasn't sure of that at all. Everything sounded delicious and exotic: *prosciutto con melone, cannelloni, saltimbocca*—she could have ordered them all without even asking what they were. But pizza was what he'd offered and it would be what she accepted. Suddenly, it seemed terribly important to keep the parameters of the next hour clearly defined.

'Yes,' she said, folding the menu and setting it aside. 'I'm quite sure.'

She watched as he signalled to the waiter and ordered, surprised at first to realise that he was speaking in what sounded like a fluent stream of Italian. But then she thought that nothing about Seth Richards should surprise her any more. She'd seen a side of him today that she'd never seen before.

It seemed to be taking an awfully long time just to order pizza. And the look on his face was so serious—

the waiter's face, as well. Kristin fought back a smile. Pizza, for heaven's sake! Who'd have dreamed the estimable Mr Richards liked pizza? In all these months, if anyone had suggested it, she'd have laughed. Seth Richards was the sort of man who dined on steaks and prime ribs of beef at The Palm, or *coquilles St-Jacques* at Lutece. She'd made reservations for him there, and at similar restaurants, dozens of times over the past months. But pizza, in a little place like this?

And yet, he looked completely at home here. He seemed relaxed, open, he seemed...

'What's that smile for?'

Kristin gave herself a mental shake. 'What smile?' she said.

He grinned. 'The one that makes you look like Mona Lisa's stand-in. You were looking at me with such a strange expression on your face.'

She blushed. 'Was I?' she said, looking down at her napkin. 'I—I was listening to you talk with the waiter. That was Italian, wasn't it?'

He laughed. 'Or what passes for Italian. I haven't really spoken it in years, except to New York waiters who know which side their tip is buttered on.'

'Was your family Italian?'

He shook his head. 'No. I picked the language up bouncing around Europe the year after I graduated college.'

Kristin smiled. 'That must have been wonderful.'

'Yeah, it was. Just me and my backpack.' He grinned again. 'A last farewell to youth before I stepped into the cold, cruel world.'

She nodded. Only a few hours ago, it would have been hard to picture Seth Richards bumming his way across Europe. Now, she could easily imagine him doing just that. The navy pin-striped suit would have to go, of course, and the tie, but that was easy enough. She could see him now in faded jeans and an equally faded shirt, the sleeves rolled up to his forearms, the first buttons undone...

'What are you thinking?'

Kristin blushed darkly. 'Nothing,' she said quickly. 'I just—I...' She swallowed hard. 'I've always been sorry I didn't learn to speak another language. My grandmother tried to teach me, but...'

'Swedish?'

She looked at him dumbly. 'What?'

'Norwegian, then. Or Danish. Your first name is Scandinavian isn't it? Kristin?'

Her breath caught. It was the first time he'd ever said her name. She thought, with a sudden incredulity, that she'd never heard it sound quite like that—softer, somehow, and gentler.

'No,' she said. 'I mean, yes, I suppose it is. But I'm not. I'm this mad brew of Welsh and English and Swiss.'

Seth laughed, his teeth very straight and white against his tan. 'All that?'

She nodded. 'Along with touches of American Indian. I've a great-great-grandmother who was Sioux. At least, that's the story the family likes to tell.'

His eyes moved slowly over her face, moving at last to her dark hair.

'Yes,' he said, his smile fading, 'I can see it now. Your hair is as dark as the night sky.' His eyes met hers, and a little furrow appeared between his brows, as if he were puzzled. 'Funny,' he said, 'but I never noticed before.'

Kristin's heart rose in her throat. He was looking at her so strangely, almost as if he were seeing her for the first time. And she—and she...

'The *vino*, *signore*, just as you requested. A chianti classico. I think you'll like it.'

She looked up, grateful for the interruption. Their waiter was standing beside the table, holding a bottle of wine for Seth's approval.

'Wine? But you said——'

'I said we'd have pizza, and so we shall,' he said with a quick smile. The waiter opened the bottle, poured some into a glass, and offered it. Kristin watched as Seth sniffed it, tasted it, and nodded his agreement. 'But pizza goes better with *vino*, isn't that right, Arturo?'

The waiter nodded as he filled their glasses. When he'd gone, Seth lifted his.

'A toast,' he said. 'To Miss Marshall, who has the patience of a saint.'

Kristin laughed. 'Thank you. But it's not true.'

He raised one dark brow. 'Actually, I didn't think so. Sometimes there's a rather bloodthirsty glare behind all those very proper "yes, Mr Richards" and "of course, Mr Richards."'

She laughed again. 'It's not true.'

He took a sip of wine, then put down the glass and stared at her, a bemused expression on his face. 'No,' he said softly, 'it's not. How do you put up with me, Miss Marshall? Mrs Dowd tells me I'm not the easiest man to work for.'

'I haven't complained,' she said quickly.

He smiled. 'You came close this morning.' His smile dimmed. 'Not that I blame you. I was pretty rough on you, and I apologise.'

'It isn't necessary. I understand.'

His mouth twisted. 'No, you don't,' he said. 'But it's nice of you to let me off the hook so easily.' His eyes met hers again, then slid away. 'Come on, taste your wine. Tell me if you like it.'

Kristin lifted the glass and slipped at the deep burgundy liquid. The wine was warm and tart, and it filled her mouth with the taste of faraway places.

'Yes,' she said. 'I like it very much.'

Seth smiled. 'Good.' They sat in silence for a few moments, and then he shifted in his seat. 'Have you ever worn it loose?'

'Worn it . . .'

'Your hair.' His glance moved over her again. 'Have you ever worn it down? To the office, I mean.'

She swallowed past the lump that had suddenly risen in her throat. 'No. No, I haven't.'

He nodded. 'I didn't think you had. I'd have remembered if...' His words trailed away and he cleared his throat. 'Well,' he said briskly, 'here's our pizza. With mushrooms and sausage, as requested.'

They ate silently for the next few minutes. At least, Kristin went through the motions of eating. But she might as well have been biting into cardboard. The pizza was probably delicious: it smelled wonderful, and it looked as good as any she'd ever seen.

But each mouthful lodged in her throat. She was conscious only of the man seated opposite her. Suddenly, her whirling mind seemed determined to imprint each detail of his face into memory. She had always known his eyes were hazel, but never that they were green when he tilted his head a certain way. And his mouth—why had she thought it narrow? His lower lip was full, and there was a tiny indentation just below it that mirrored the cleft in his chin...

'...better than in Italy,' he said.

She looked up helplessly. 'Did you—did you say something?'

He nodded. 'I said that American pizza is the best in the world. Better than what you get in Italy, that's for sure.'

Kristin lifted her shoulders, then lowered them again. 'I wouldn't know. I've never been anywhere.'

'Ah. Well, then, you'll enjoy the Bahamas.'

She stared at him. 'The Bahamas?'

Seth smiled. 'Yes. Your trip next week. Remember?'

'My...' She touched her tongue to her lips. 'Oh. That.'

His eyebrows rose. 'You don't sound very excited about it, Miss Marshall.'

'Well, I—I...' She put down her fork and folded her hands in her lap. 'I've been thinking about that, Mr Richards. And—and it's not vital that I go. In fact, I'm perfectly willing to change my plans, if it helps.'

He lifted his glass to his lips and sipped at the wine, his eyes steady on hers.

'What about your friend?' he asked finally.

'My friend?'

'Yes. Won't he be disappointed?'

'No. I mean, you're wrong about...' She fell silent. You're wrong about that, she'd almost said, it isn't a 'he', it's a 'she'. But suddenly his face changed, and she saw seated opposite her not Seth Richards but the man who had betrayed her trust after using her years before.

Kristin blinked. No. Seth Richards wasn't like that. He always kept a careful distance between himself and the women who worked for him; hadn't poor Linda learned that the hard way?

Besides, what would he want with her? He could have any woman he wanted—well, almost any. One had turned him down today, although she couldn't imagine why the woman had been so foolish...

Kristin's fork dropped from her hand and clattered against the plate.

'Miss Marshall?' She looked up. Seth leaned across the table towards her. 'Are you all right?'

'Yes. Yes, I'm fine. I'm just—I guess I'm more tired than I'd realised.'

He frowned. 'Of course,' he said, pushing back his chair and rising to his feet. 'Forgive me.'

She smiled shakily as she stood up. 'Thank you for dinner, Mr Richards. It was delicious.'

Out on the pavement, Seth suddenly put his hand lightly on Kristin's arm.

'You never answered my question,' he said.

She looked up at him. 'Your question?'

His gaze fixed on her face. 'If you cancel your trip to the Bahamas, won't your friend be upset?'

She took a deep breath. 'Yes. But—but we can take our trip at some later date. It's not a problem.'

His eyes darkened, as if someone had shut off a light.

'In that case,' he said, 'I would appreciate it if you'd put it off, yes.'

Kristin nodded. 'No problem, Mr Richards. I can— did I say something funny?'

Seth shook his head. But she could see that he was smiling.

'It just seems strange to hear you call me "Mr Richards", Miss Marshall, considering that I'm about to tell you that you have a bit of melted cheese on your chin.'

Kristin's hand flew to her face. 'Where? Is it...?'

'Right there,' he said gently. He touched his finger to her chin. A tremor went through her, but she forced herself to remain absolutely still.

'Thank you, Mr Richards.'

'You're welcome, Miss Marshall.'

Now, sitting in the kitchen and remembering, Kristin wondered which of them had been the first to smile. Seth, she thought, and then she shook her head. No, it had been she—well, one of them certainly had, and the smiles had turned to easy laughter.

'Miss Marshall,' he'd said with great formality, 'I think that even Mrs Dowd would approve of my calling you "Kristin" after six months of working side by side. Do you agree?'

And she'd laughed and said yes, she thought that would be fine. And that was when he'd said good, it was about time, and he would much prefer it if she were to call him "Seth".

'No,' she'd answered quickly, 'I couldn't do that.'

'Why not?' he'd asked pleasantly, and for the life of her Kristin hadn't been able to come up with a single intelligent reason. After all, this was an informal world. And many of the secretaries at Harbrace International were on a first-name basis with their bosses. In fact, now that she thought about it, the formality she and Seth had followed all these months was probably the exception and not the rule.

'All right,' she'd said shyly. 'Seth it is.'

His smile had dazzled her. 'I'm glad to hear it, Kristin.'

And that had been all. Kristin sighed now as she got to her feet and shut off the kitchen light. Seth had hailed a passing taxi and handed her in.

She hesitated in the doorway to her room. There had been something else, now that she thought about it. She had turned towards Seth to thank him, and she'd caught the faintest scent in the air...

Puzzled, she'd looked at him. He was smiling, pressing a bill into her hands, and she'd forgotten the elusive aroma in her determination to assure him that she'd pay her own fare.

Seth had laughed. 'If it makes you feel better, just remember that Harbrace is paying for your ride.'

It *had* made her feel better. Somehow, anything that made those couple of hours seem more like business and less like a pleasant interlude had become important.

Her cab had rolled off into the night, and Seth had headed in the other direction, towards his east-side condominium.

'Get some rest, Kristin,' had been his last words to her.

And that, she thought now as she slipped off her robe and crawled wearily into bed, was exactly what she was going to do. Lord knew she needed it—this had been the longest, strangest day that she could ever remember.

*　*　*

Hours later, just before dawn, Kristin awoke, trembling, from the depths of her recurring dream. She breathed deeply, orientating herself to the familiar walls of her bedroom, and then she lay curled on her side, her hand under her cheek, watching the sky shade from black to grey.

The dream had left her shaken. It had been so real: the man, the warmth of his embrace—even his scent. It was still with her, lingering on her skin as if—as if . . .

A soft moan of despair rose in her throat. Woodsmoke and mountain air, she thought, and her heart began to race.

That was the scent she'd tried to identify as Seth had handed her into the cab.

It was Seth's, and it always had been.

He was the man in her dream.

CHAPTER FOUR

KRISTIN lay waiting for sunlight. Like a child seeking the comfort of dawn, she kept telling herself that the new day would banish the dark imaginings of the night. Her dream would go back to being just a dream and the man in it a faceless stranger.

But the morning was sunless. In its cool autumnal light, the harsh reality of her dream became even more disturbing. How could she have harboured such fantasies about Seth without knowing it? She felt as if she had somehow betrayed herself.

Angrily, she threw off the blankets and slammed her alarm clock to premature silence. The last thing she wanted was to wake Susan. She wasn't up to any of her bright chatter this morning. Besides, who knew what might happen if her room-mate offered even one well-intentioned warning that Kristin was letting her boss take advantage of her? Her nerves were tingling. Anything might set her off and she knew she'd say things she would regret later.

She showered quickly, then dressed, forcing herself to focus on the basics of her morning routine, as if by clinging to them she could banish everything else from her mind. The beige wool suit, she thought, peering into her wardrobe. Or perhaps the navy—yes, that was better. And a white silk blouse, along with a blue and red scarf at her throat for colour.

But the ruse didn't work very well: she found herself caught in a slow-motion parody of dressing. It took long minutes to decide between equally discreet gold button

earrings and ones made of silver when her thoughts kept
slipping away to Seth and to the dream.

Crazy. It was crazy, all of it. Kristin sat down at her
dressing-table and stared into the mirror. She had never
once looked at her boss the way a woman looked at a
man. He was Mr Richards, her employer. That was how
she'd always thought of him—until yesterday. But the
dreams hadn't begun then; she'd had them for a long
time now. For weeks...

'Stop that nonsense!'

Her voice hissed in the silence. Quickly, Kristin lifted
her hair from her face and pulled it back. It really was
too long and heavy; cutting it seemed a better and better
idea. Tomorrow, then, or...

Her fingers stilled. What was it Seth had said last
night? That he'd never noticed the colour of her hair
before; yes, that was it. Well, then, he had never thought
of her in any way except as his secretary, a faceless drone
who answered his phone and typed his letters. The
efficient Miss Marshall.

Kristin closed her eyes. Not any more, she wasn't. She
was Kristin now, and he was Seth. And what he'd said
last evening was that her hair was the colour of the night;
she could still remember the softness in his voice, the
look of faint surprise on his face, as if he were seeing
her for the first time.

Her eyes flew open. Enough, she thought, giving
herself a mental shake. She was making mountains out
of molehills. What he'd said had been meaningless. For
all she knew, the man had never even noticed she *had*
hair. It was as if one of the machines in his office had
come to life.

She picked up her brush and attacked her hair,
brushing it back from her face with steady, harsh strokes.
As for her dreams, well, they weren't hard to explain
either. She knew what dreams were: harmless fantasies
created by an idle mind. They might be vivid, even em-

barrassing, but they certainly weren't expressions of real desire.

Hadn't Susan joked about the dream she'd had of Mel Gibson after seeing his last film?

'I'd tell you all about it, but it was X-rated,' she'd said with an exaggerated leer.

They'd both laughed, and Susan had sighed over her dream for days—but that certainly didn't mean Suze wanted to fall into Mel Gibson's arms!

The recollection made Kristin feel a little better. All she'd done, she thought as she pinned up her hair, was shape a mindless fantasy with the image closest to hand—Seth Richards. It was her own fault, really. The truth was, her love-life was sadly lacking. Paul and the other men she knew were nice enough, but there was nothing terribly exciting about any of them. They were invariably pleasant, always eager to please...

Kristin caught her bottom lip between her teeth. Paul had taken her to the theatre, to the ballet, to all the latest films and the trendiest restaurants, but she'd never enjoyed one of those evenings as much as she'd enjoyed last night.

But it was foolish to compare Paul with Seth. It was foolish to compare any of the men she dated with him. They were all nice-looking, but none of them had Seth's vibrant masculinity, or his spontaneity either. Paul would probably never think of taking her to a charming restaurant for something as homely as pizza, and he certainly wouldn't order an obviously expensive bottle of wine to go with it.

And Paul had never said her hair was the colour of the night, he'd never...

A tremor went through her. God, what was she thinking? Of course it was foolish to compare Paul and Seth. She'd had her fill of men who were larger than life, who charmed women with soft words and promises of forever after. Moonlight and roses led to disaster, especially when the man doling out the moonlight and roses was the man you worked for, and when the end came your job and your pride were gone, too.

Kristin lifted her chin as she stared at her reflection.

'You, my girl, are going to make the most of that week off the boss offered you next month,' she said aloud in a clear, firm voice. 'And after six or seven days of lying on the beach, the only things you'll dream about will be the sea and the sand.'

She nodded sternly, then switched off the lamp on her dressing-table and marched to the door.

By the time she reached work, she was feeling much better. Still, she was glad that Seth would be in Boston all day. A day's reprieve couldn't hurt—by the time she saw him tomorrow, she'd be fine. All this craziness would be behind her.

The morning passed quickly. The office was quiet with him gone; there was time to type some letters and update the files. At one o'clock, she had her lunch at her desk, as she often did, one eye on her container of raspberry yogurt and the other on a new romantic paperback she was halfway through.

By mid-afternoon, her convictions of the morning had begun to slip, and her thoughts turned to dreams and their meanings. Susan had fantasised about a movie star, something lots of women probably did. Well, if you were into fantasy lovers, that made sense. It was exciting but it was safe. Mel Gibson wasn't about to walk into your life, was he?

She paused, her fingers suddenly still on the typewriter keyboard. But she—she had dreamed about a man she knew, a man she worked with five days a week. Wasn't that dangerous, especially since she had never had dreams that intimate before? There was something distressing about that, something...

'Damn!'

The paper coming out of the typewriter was hardly legible. The ribbon, Kristin thought. It needed changing—and that was a job she hated, even though it was supposedly easy to do.

With a sigh, she rose and opened the machine. It was new; she had never peered inside it before. Nothing looked familiar at all. She pulled open her desk drawer and poked inside until she found a replacement ribbon and the instruction booklet that had come with the typewriter.

Yes, there it was. There was something to depress, something else to pull, and then—so the booklet claimed—the ribbon cartridge would lift neatly out.

But it didn't. Kristin poked and pushed, and still the thing refused to budge. Flustered, annoyed at herself for her mechanical ineptitude, she straightened up finally, slapped her hands on her hips, and glared at the typewriter.

'You're nothing but a useless piece of junk,' she said. 'If you don't come out of there right now, I'm going to kick you to kingdom come!'

Soft laughter drifted towards her from across the room. Startled, she looked up—and saw Seth standing in the open doorway.

Her heart gave an unaccustomed leap. The cool weather had brought a flush to his cheeks, and the wind had ruffled his hair so that it lay in silken disarray across his forehead. Her heart did a funny little turn again as she wondered how long he'd been watching her.

He was smiling, and she ached to smile in return. Instead, she assumed what she hoped was a professional expression of neutrality.

'Good afternoon, Mr Richards,' she said, amazed at how calm she sounded when her pulse was racing. 'I didn't expect you to come back to the office today.'

His brows rose at the way she'd addressed him, but he said nothing about it. Instead, he nodded at the typewriter.

'Would you like me to do that for you?' His smile became a grin. 'Or would you rather go another round with it on your own?'

'It's new,' she said defensively. 'The ribbon goes in differently. It...' She fell silent. 'Yes,' she said after a moment, 'if you wouldn't mind, I'd be very grateful.'

He shrugged out of his coat as he walked towards her and dropped it carelessly across the back of her chair.

'Here,' he said, holding out his hand, 'give me the cartridge.'

Their fingers brushed, and an electric shock raced along Kristin's skin. She jumped, and their eyes met. Seth gave her a slow smile.

'Sorry. It must be the weather. I'm full of electricity today.'

She nodded and dragged her gaze from his. 'It's cold out,' she said in a choked voice.

He hesitated, and then he cleared his throat. 'Yes. The first real fall day we've had.' She looked up as he bent over the open typewriter. 'Let me see. I think if we just push this—and then that...' The ribbon popped out easily. 'And then fit the new one in like so...' The cartridge clicked into place, and Seth straightened up and smiled at her. 'Done.'

Kristin nodded. 'Thank you.' She looked at him and then she turned away quickly and began straightening her desk. 'I'm afraid I've never been very good with mechanical things.'

He laughed again. 'That's all right, Kristin. I know it's a terribly chauvinistic view, but men rarely expect pretty women to be able to handle anything more complicated than a can opener.'

The remark brought a rush of pink to her cheeks. So, she thought, it had started already. One simple meal, a little pleasant conversation, and now he thought he could start a flirtation with her. Her brain worked furiously to come up with some cold rejoinder that would stop the nonsense before it began. She looked up, eyes flashing—and found Seth busily sorting through the mail on her desk, completely unaware of her presence.

Kristin closed her eyes. She'd over-reacted. What he'd said had been a throw-away remark, that was all. Pretty women, he'd said, which definitely put her into a category shared with untold others. It wasn't as if he'd called her beautiful or given her a special compliment.

Was she pretty, compared to the women he knew? Did he really think of her that way? It would be nice to think so, it would be...

Her eyes flew open and she turned away, trembling. What was the matter with her? First, she wanted him to notice her, and then she didn't. But you couldn't have it both ways. Either he saw her as he always had, or...

'Kristin?' She drew a deep breath and turned towards Seth. He frowned as their eyes met. 'Is anything wrong?'

She smiled politely. 'I was—I was just thinking that I'd better finish typing up that report I was transcribing. Unless you've something else you want done first?'

He sighed. Suddenly she could see how tired he looked.

'Yes,' he said, 'if you can spare the time, there *is* something I'd like to talk to you about. Come into my office, will you?'

She nodded, watching in silence as he collected his things, then walked into the adjoining room. After a moment, she picked up her pad and pencil and followed him.

Seth was sitting at his desk, going through his mail. He looked up distractedly.

'Sit down, Kristin.' He shook his head when he saw her open her notebook. 'You won't need that,' he said. He watched her in silence, and then he smiled. 'I gather you got home safely last night.'

She nodded again. 'Yes, thank you.'

'Good. It occurred to me afterwards that I really should have seen you to your door. In this crazy city...'

Her brain conjured up a picture of Seth standing close beside her in the narrow lift in her apartment building. The hall that led to her door was long and dimly lit; at that hour of the night, it would have been silent. Their footsteps would have echoed loudly, hers quick and light, his steady and sure. Once at the door, Seth would have smiled at her and she'd have smiled back and thanked him for a pleasant evening, and then—and then...

'No,' she said sharply. Seth stared at her, and she swallowed hard. 'I mean—it wasn't necessary. I live in a very safe apartment building. The outside door is always locked and you have to buzz to get in, and...' Kristin clamped her lips together. She was rambling on like a fool. She drew a deep breath and shifted in her chair. 'You said there was something you wanted to tell me,' she said.

Seth looked at her. 'Yes,' he said after a pause, 'that's right. There is.'

He rose slowly, looked down at her, then ran his hand through his hair. Something was troubling him, Kristin thought suddenly. The gesture told her so. And now he was walking to the window, staring out at the city, his hands jammed into his trouser pockets. Yes. There was definitely something on his mind. He always looked out of the window that way when he needed a solution for a delicate situation.

She stared at him. How did she know that? Just yesterday, Susan had questioned her about Seth and she'd assured her in all honesty that she really knew nothing about the man, except his cadence when dictating.

And that had been the truth. Only a day ago, Kristin would have been hard-pressed even to describe the colour of his eyes.

But she knew the colour now. His back was to her, but she knew his eyes were hazel, that when he was distressed—as he seemed to be now—they turned a chocolate-brown.

Kristin put her hand to her throat. When had she learned all this? Surely not overnight. Had she, somehow, been storing up information about him? The girls she'd left behind in the steno pool had even teased her about how little she knew about her new boss.

'What's he like?' they'd asked eagerly.

'A hard worker,' Kristin had said, and they'd groaned with dismay.

'Who cares about that?' they'd said. 'What's he like as a man?'

She had been unable to come up with an answer, and after a while, they'd given up asking.

But she could come up with one now, she thought uneasily. She could tell them that he touched his tongue to his lip when he was deep in thought, and that his eyes crinkled when he smiled. She could tell them that his hair was just a little longer than it should be, that it curled at the nape of his neck, just brushing his collar. She could tell them that in the sweltering heat of an August day, when the air-conditioning system had given up in defeat, he had taken off his suit jacket, rolled up the sleeves of his white shirt and undone his tie. She had seen the dark whorl of hair showing at his open collar, seen the knotted muscles in his forearms...

Kristin's chair squealed in protest as she shoved it back and got quickly to her feet. Seth turned towards her, frowning.

'I—I...' She stared at him helplessly. 'I have work to do, Mr Richards. So, if you don't mind...'

His eyes swept over her face. 'I thought we'd agreed it would be Kristin and Seth from now on.'

She swallowed. 'We did. But I—I'm not comfortable calling you... It just doesn't seem right.'

A muscle knotted in his jaw. 'It seems very right to me,' he said.

She stared at him, searching for some hidden meaning in the simply spoken words. But his face was expressionless. After a moment, he turned away.

'Sit down, Kristin,' he said. 'Please.'

She did, sinking back slowly into her chair. There was a hollow feeling in the pit of her stomach. She felt, suddenly, as if she were a little girl sitting in the dental chair, waiting for the kiss of the drill.

If only she could go back and erase yesterday, she thought feverishly. If only she hadn't agreed to let Seth take her to supper. It had been like—like opening Pandora's box, and now she was struggling to get the lid back on and keep it shut before...

'This apartment of yours,' he said abruptly.

She looked up, startled. He was leaning against his desk, his hazel eyes fixed on her.

'Yes?'

He cleared his throat. 'Do you own it? Is it a condominium?'

Kristin laughed. The unexpected question was so far from anything she'd been thinking that she couldn't help herself.

'No,' she said, 'it's a rental. Actually, we live in fear of the building going condo. We could never afford——'

'We.' Seth's voice was flat. 'Of course. Your roommate. Have you and he—have you been together long?'

A flush rose to her cheeks. She had forgotten he thought she lived with a man.

'I don't——'

Kristin's mouth snapped shut. Why was she correcting him? Let him think she lived with someone. Maybe the self-protective lie would keep her safe from whatever lunacy seemed to be seizing her.

'I don't remember, exactly. About six months, I think.'

His brows drew together in a frown. 'You think?' His voice was cool. 'Aren't you sure?'

She shrugged her shoulders. 'Yes. Six months,' she said, her voice as cool as his, even though her pulse was galloping. Where was all this leading?

Seth nodded. 'Not very long, then.'

'Mr Richards—Seth—I'm afraid I don't see...'

'And are you...?' He frowned again. 'I don't know quite how to say this,' he said, looking past her to the wall. 'Are you committed to each other?'

Kristin blinked. 'Are we...?'

Seth cleared his throat. 'Hell,' he said roughly, 'I don't know what term you use. Dedicated. Damn it, Kristin, you know what I mean.'

'Yes,' she said, her flush deepening, 'I do. And I don't think it's any of your——'

'Are you?' he demanded.

She hesitated. 'No,' she said finally. 'Not—not in the way you mean.'

His mouth thinned. 'I'm not surprised,' he said coldly. 'That seems to be the way young women are today. They form liaisons without caring what anyone thinks, without much thought for the future. They——'

The clipped, furious words stopped in mid-sentence. Seth stared at her, and then he uttered a short sharp oath and stalked across the room.

Kristin watched him in stunned silence. Whatever was happening was beyond her comprehension. She had never heard him curse before. And he'd never asked her a personal question. As for the lecture on morality, it had shaken her to the bone—especially since she didn't deserve it. Perhaps she'd been wrong to let him think she lived with a man. Perhaps...

'Kristin.' Seth turned towards her, his face unreadable. 'I'm sorry,' he said curtly. 'You're quite right; the way you lead your life is none of my business.'

She swallowed hard. There it was again, that little jab at her morality. She couldn't let him think that about her.

'Mr Richards,' she said, 'Seth—I think—I think I should explain something. My room-mate——'

'When you took this job, was it explained to you that it might involve some travel?'

Puzzled, she nodded. 'Yes, Mrs Dowd said there might be an occasional——'

'It was one of the reasons I approved her selection of you. Your personnel file said you were unencumbered.'

'I am,' she said, before she could think. 'I mean, I——'

'I know what you mean,' he said with a cold grimness. 'In which case, you should have no difficulty with my next question.' He paused, and then he crossed his arms and stared at her. 'What if I asked you to give up your flat?'

Kristin stared at him. 'What?'

His jaw tightened. 'You heard me,' he said in a voice that was almost a growl. 'What would you do if I asked you to leave your apartment—and that room-mate of yours?'

'You have absolutely no right to——'

'Just answer the question.'

She drew a deep breath as she pushed back her chair and got to her feet. So, she thought, she hadn't been wrong a few minutes ago—but this wasn't any little flirtation Seth Richards had in mind when he'd said she was pretty. It was something far more specific. And that nonsense about the way she lived hadn't been about morality. He hadn't been passing judgement on her, he'd simply been annoyed that someone else had got there first.

You had to give him credit for being brazen. It had taken Vincent Chalmers weeks to get this far. But Seth Richards had bypassed the preliminaries and gone

straight to the point. He had taken her reaction to one
pleasant evening and come up with what had once delicately been called a proposition.

So much for the formalities of the past six months.
And so much for decency. Did he think she was so
dazzled to have finally caught his eye that she'd be a
push-over? Did he think she'd forget that only yesterday
he'd been hot to bed another woman who...

Soft laughter sounded from the doorway. Startled,
Kristin span towards the sound. A woman stood in the
open doorway, watching them both. She was small, delicately boned, with a short, shiny cap of glossy chestnut
hair. She smiled as she walked into the room.

'I would have knocked,' she said amiably, 'but the
door was open. I hope I'm not intruding.'

Kristin looked at Seth, watching in silence as his eyes
darkened, then narrowed.

'Jeanne,' he said in a tight voice. 'What a surprise.'

Jeanne. Jeanne Lester? Dumbfounded, Kristin stared
from him to the woman.

The woman smiled and stopped beside Kristin. 'Hello,'
she said, as if she'd somehow heard her thoughts. 'I'm
Jeanne Lester.' She held out her hand. 'You must be
Kristin.'

Kristin accepted the outstretched hand slowly. 'Yes,'
she said finally, 'I am.'

'Well, it's nice to meet you.' She turned her smile on
Seth, whose expression had not changed. 'I suppose I
should have telephoned. But I was in the neighbourhood, and I just thought I'd drop by and see if you
were free for tea.'

Seth glowered at her, and then his face softened. 'That
sounds fine,' he said. 'I'm glad you did.'

Kristin stared at him in amazement while a cold rage
built within her. How dared he stand there, smiling at
Jeanne Lester, when just a few minutes ago he'd been

blatantly trying to...to...? He didn't even have the decency to be embarrassed.

And to think she'd even imagined this man to be attractive or desirable.

She drew herself up. 'I'll be at my desk if you need me,' she said coldly.

She turned away and started towards the door, but Seth's voice stopped her.

'Kristin.'

She looked back at him. 'Yes, Mr Richards?'

His eyes were cool. 'I'm still waiting for your answer.'

Colour rose into her cheeks. He couldn't mean...

'I know it's unexpected, but the transfer came through very suddenly.'

Kristin stared at him. 'Transfer?'

Seth nodded. 'Exactly. I've been assigned to the Rome office for a few months, and the company's agreed that I should take my secretary with me.'

She felt the floor tilt beneath her feet. 'Your secretary?' she said, parroting his words. 'Is that why—is that what you meant about giving up my flat? Because you want me to go to Rome with you?'

He scowled. 'Of course.'

Jeanne Lester laughed softly. 'I don't suppose it's occurred to you that she might prefer to stay here, in the States?'

Seth glared at her. 'Not everyone is foolish enough to turn down a trip abroad, Jeanne.'

'We've already settled this, Seth,' the woman said calmly 'I didn't come here to argue.'

His glare deepened, and he thrust his hands into his pockets and turned to the window.

'On second thoughts, I don't feel much like tea, Jeanne. I've a lot of work to finish up.'

Jeanne's smile faded. 'I understand,' she said softly. She looked at his stiff back as if she wanted to say something more and then turned quickly away and walked to the door. 'Goodbye,' she said to Kristin, 'it was nice meeting you.'

The door shut quietly after her. For a moment, Kristin stood staring at it, and then she cleared her throat.

'If you don't need me any longer...'

'Damn it, Kristin.' Seth's voice was harsh with barely suppressed anger as he turned from the window. 'What do I have to do to get an answer out of you?'

Kristin swallowed. Rome. He wanted an answer about Rome, but she couldn't give him one. Not now, not so quickly. Too many things had happened. She'd gone from liking him to hating him to—to...

To what? What did she feel for Seth Richards? A little while ago, she'd been ready to quit her job when she thought he was propositioning her.

Now, knowing he hadn't meant that at all and that he'd apparently asked Jeanne Lester to accompany him to Rome, her anger had been replaced by something else, something that had begun as a formless heaviness in her breast and was rapidly becoming a sharp pain in her heart.

God. What was happening to her?

'I'll have to take up the reins quickly.' Kristin blinked and stared at Seth. He was watching her with impatience stamped across his face. 'There'll be no time to set up an office routine. You know how I work, Kristin, how I want things done.'

She knew, with a sudden cold insight, that she could not go with him. The assignment was a plum—only a day or two ago, she'd have jumped at the opportunity.

But everything had changed. Now, the thought of being far from home with him frightened her. Without the touchstones of her life around her, who knew what might happen?

'Kristin?' His voice was cold, almost contemptuous. 'I need your answer now.'

'No,' she said, so sharply and swiftly that her voice sounded as if it belonged to a stranger. 'No,' she repeated more carefully, 'I can't go with you.'

'The company will pay for your travel and lodging,' he said, as if she hadn't spoken. He waited, his face cold and hard. 'Well?' he said finally. 'What's your decision?'

'I already gave you my answer. Thank you for asking me, but I can't accept the assignment.'

A cool smile flickered across his face. 'Because?' he said in a soft, ominous voice.

She forced herself to smile politely and meet his gaze head-on.

'Because,' she said calmly, 'I have commitments here.'

His mouth narrowed. 'I thought you had no commitments.'

She felt her cheeks grow warm. 'I didn't say that, exactly. What I said was——'

A look of distaste swept across his face. 'Please,' he said, striding past her to his desk, 'don't bother.'

'I'm just trying to make you see that——'

'I told you, the way you live is none of my business.'

Kristin drew herself up. 'No,' she said with frigid self-control, 'it most certainly is not.'

'Whether you take the assignment or not is, of course, your prerogative.' His eyes met hers. 'But before you reach a final decision, I suggest you call Personnel and ask Mrs Dowd if there are any openings you could fill.' His lips drew back from his teeth in a smile that was not a smile at all. 'Who knows? She may be able to get you your old spot in the steno pool.'

The mockery in his tone infuriated her. But before she could think of a response, he sat down behind his desk, picked up some papers, and swivelled his chair towards the window.

It was a classic—and contemptuous—dismissal.

CHAPTER FIVE

AT LEAST something good had come out of this mess, Kristin thought as she slammed her desk drawer. She was over her silly infatuation with Seth Richards. In fact, she wondered why she'd ever been attracted to him at all. He was the kind of man she despised, a man who thought that a woman would be happy to dance to his tune. And when she didn't, the polite veneer that he showed the world slipped away and he turned into a ruthless bastard who'd do anything to get his own way.

She felt almost sorry for Jeanne Lester. As for herself, well, Seth Richards didn't run Harbrace. She was a damned good secretary. What kind of difficulty could there possibly be in finding another place for her in the company?

The director of Personnel greeted Kristin pleasantly and listened to her with no change of expression. When she finished, Mrs Dowd nodded and sat back in her chair.

'No,' she said, 'of course you don't have to accept the transfer, Miss Marshall.'

Kristin let out her breath. Despite all the reassurances she'd made to herself, hearing those calmly spoken words from Mrs Dowd herself made all the difference. She smiled gratefully.

'I didn't think so. Thank you for confirming it.'

The older woman's lips pursed. 'But I did ask you about travel assignments when you were interviewed. My notes are right here. You said you'd have no difficulty with travel.'

'Well, yes,' Kristin said warily. 'But I thought you meant a day or two in the branch offices. I never dreamed you were talking about...'

Mrs Dowd looked at her sternly. 'I don't like seeing my match-ups fail, you know. It took me some time to find just the right girl to suit Mr Richards, and now I'll have to go through the entire procedure again.'

Kristin stared at her. She could feel the atmosphere chilling. None of this is my fault, she wanted to say, it's all your precious Seth Richards' doing. He's a smug, cold-hearted bastard.

But she knew better. Seth was an executive, and she was merely his secretary. So she swallowed the angry words and managed what she hoped was a contrite smile.

'I'm sorry if I've caused you any difficulty,' she said politely. She waited for the personnel director to speak; when she didn't, Kristin cleared her throat. 'Mrs Dowd? I wonder if you could tell me what openings I might fill after Mr Richards leaves for Rome?'

The older woman frowned and pulled a box of file cards towards her. 'Let's see,' she said, thumbing through them rapidly. She paused and pulled one out. 'Here's something. One of the secretaries in the law department has given notice.' She looked up, her frown deepening. 'But you're not a legal secretary, are you?'

'No. But I could learn. I——'

'I'm afraid it's a position that needs someone with considerable experience.' The head of Personnel peered down at the file cards again. 'Accounting needs a book-keeper,' she mused, 'and a financial clerk. Of course, you wouldn't qualify for those spots, Miss Marshall.'

Kristin folded her hands tightly in her lap. 'What about secretarial positions?'

Mrs Dowd smiled politely. 'I'm afraid I don't have any.'

'Surely there must be something,' Kristin said, hating the little note of desperation that suddenly sounded in her voice.

The older woman's eyes met hers. 'Well, there is one opening,' she said. 'There's a vacancy coming up in your old department in a few days.'

Kristin blinked. 'In the steno pool, you mean?'

'Yes. You could step right into it, if you like.'

Well, she thought, that was right in line with Seth's cold prophecy.

'At what pay?' she asked with as much dignity as she could manage.

Mrs Dowd's mouth twitched in a frosty smile. 'At stenographer's pay, naturally. Harbrace doesn't pay administrative wages to clerical employees, my dear.'

Kristin nodded. She hadn't really expected any other answer.

'Well, then,' she said slowly, 'I guess I should ask what's due me upon termination.'

The head of Personnel looked up, peering at her over her half-frame glasses.

'Due you?' she repeated.

'Yes. What is my severance pay? Aside from the vacation wages coming to me, I mean.'

The older woman's brows arched. 'Why, none, Miss Marshall. You'd be leaving us of your own accord. The company's offered you employment—it's you who has refused it.'

There was nothing more to say after that. Kristin gathered herself together, thanked Mrs Dowd for her help with what she thought was admirable courtesy, and went home.

Susan was in and out all weekend, which was just as well. She wasn't ready to tell her room-mate what had happened—not yet.

It would be one thing to say she'd lost her job, but quite another to tell her the reason.

'You mean, you turned down an all-expenses-paid assignment in Rome?' Susan would demand incredulously. 'Are you nuts?'

And then Kristin would have to try and come up with some acceptable explanation because the truth was far too humiliating.

How could a grown woman admit that she'd turned down a job because she had a schoolgirl crush on her boss and it scared the life out of her?

The only consolation, Kristin told herself as she pored through the employment section of the Sunday paper, was that all that was past tense. She'd *had* a crush on Seth, but it was history.

Monday morning, after Susan had rushed off to work, Kristin gathered the remnants of her courage together and telephoned her office.

Seth answered on the first ring. 'Where in hell are you?' he demanded as soon as he heard her voice.

She glanced at her watch. It was barely nine. 'At home,' she said evenly. 'I called to tell you that I won't be in today.'

There was a silence, and then she heard the rasp of his breath. 'Are you ill?'

'No, I'm not. I'm taking one of the vacation days coming to me. I have some personal business to attend to.'

Seth grunted. 'Thank you for giving me so much advance notice,' he said, his words cold with sarcasm.

Kristin yearned to tell him that she was only extending to him the same courtesy he had shown her. But she wasn't a fool. Every instinct warned her that it would be impossible to win a verbal contest with him.

Her fingers curled tightly around the telephone cord.

'I'm sorry if I've inconvenienced you,' she said. 'There's nothing urgent on my desk. When I get in tomorrow...'

Her words trailed away. He had already hung up. Kristin stared at the phone, then put it back in its cradle. Amazing, she thought, but somehow he had managed to make her the villain.

Well, she thought, opening the newspaper to the employment ads she'd circled, there were other jobs. New York was a big city.

By day's end, she had sat for a series of depressingly similar interviews.

'It's not your credentials, Miss Marshall, it's your lack of experience. You've only been an executive secretary for six months.'

'Yes,' she kept saying. 'But I've worked at the same company for the past five years, and——'

'I'm afraid we can't offer you anywhere near your current salary. If you can accept a pay cut for a few months...'

But it was always a considerable pay cut—one she couldn't possibly afford, not with her share of the rent hanging over her head.

At work the next day, Seth stopped beside her desk. 'What have you decided about the overseas assignment?'

Kristin looked up in surprise. 'I told you—I'm staying here.'

A cool, almost sly smile played across his mouth. 'Not quite here, Kristin. Mrs Dowd tells me you enquired and that there aren't any openings for executive secretaries.'

'I meant that I'm staying in New York. There are other companies besides this one.'

His eyes raked over her, dark with some emotion she couldn't identify.

'I trust your lover is grateful you've turned down this opportunity for him.'

The remark caught her off balance, but she recovered quickly.

'He is,' she said with a touch of defiance, and then she looked back at her desk, keeping her gaze steady until at last Seth walked away.

She would never tell him the truth about her room-mate. Let Seth Richards think she'd given up an assignment with him so she could stay in New York with another man.

It was a poor excuse for victory in this ugly little war, but it was the only one she had.

A faint plume of steam rose from the mug of coffee in Kristin's hands. She blew lightly on the dark liquid, took a careful sip, then set the mug down next to a plate of scrambled eggs which had congealed into a rubbery yellow mass. Shuddering, she pushed the plate aside.

So much for dinner, she thought, and she sighed. Well, at least she'd made the attempt. Coming into the empty flat a little while ago, she'd gone through all the usual end-of-day motions, hanging away her clothes, changing into jeans and a cotton shirt, even preparing her solitary meal.

She'd hoped that all those mundane things were talismans which might somehow restore a semblance of normality to her life and give her the courage to face what came next.

It hadn't worked. Her eyes kept straying to the wall clock, her ears kept picking up every sound. Susan would be home soon, and then, finally, Kristin would have to tell her room-mate the truth.

She had delayed the moment as long as possible. But time was closing in on her. Seth was leaving for Italy soon. And when he did, she would join the city's legion of the unemployed.

She sighed again as she lifted the coffee mug and took another swallow. She had no doubts about the choice she'd made. Turning down the transfer was the right thing to have done, she was sure of that. It was just that it would have made all the difference in her life if there'd been some warning before things came crashing down around her. Then she wouldn't be walking around with this tight feeling in her stomach, this knot of tension that wouldn't go away.

Five years ago, she'd stepped off the bus that had brought her East from Oklahoma, clutching a cheap suitcase and seeking a new life far from the memory of the man who had betrayed her. It had been a cool spring day, and, as she'd craned her neck and stared up at New York's towering skyscrapers, all her dreams had seemed possible. After all, she was young—only a year out of school—and she was eager to succeed.

But Kristin had learned quickly that girls who'd graduated first in their business class, girls who spoke quietly, who dressed discreetly, who typed and took dictation at dazzling speeds, were a dime a dozen in Manhattan.

She'd been down to her last few dollars when she'd finally landed a job, then found a cramped space in an equally cramped flat. It had taken years to work up to a good job and this flat—and now she'd lost the one and the other might well slip away from her if she wasn't careful.

No, she thought, nothing like that would happen. She'd come a long way from those difficult early days, and she wouldn't slide back. It was true, there hadn't been any job offers so far. But she hadn't been able to go for many interviews, either. Seth had made it clear that he wouldn't tolerate her taking any more days off.

She sighed and ran her finger around the rim of her coffee-cup. She'd get a job, eventually. A good one. It was just that it would take time—and on these mean streets, time was a luxury granted to very few.

She took a last swallow of coffee, then rose to her feet and walked to the sink. But she could manage—with Susan's help. All Suze had to do was say she'd carry the rent alone for a month or two.

She should have told Susan what had happened days ago. And she would have—it wasn't that she'd avoided it. Not exactly. It was just that Susan hadn't been home much lately. She'd flown off to Denver and then who knew where, and in between she'd been out to dinner and out shopping and—and . . .

Kristin groaned softly and put her hands to her head. The truth was that she *had* avoided telling Susan. At first, it had been because she didn't want to get drawn into a discussion about the Rome assignment. Now it was because she was going to be broke, which meant she was about to violate what the two women laughingly called 'The Big Taboo'.

Actually, it was the only taboo. Right from the start, they'd agreed. You could borrow clothing, beg off household chores, even use up the last of the milk for your coffee and get away with it.

But you couldn't borrow money. Ever.

'My last room-mate always needed a couple of dollars to tide her over until payday,' Susan had said right after she'd moved in. 'In the end, she owed me lots—and I hated her for making me ask for it.'

Kristin had nodded approval. 'Jane and Debbie used to argue over who owed what to whom. I'm with you on the question of money—no lending, no borrowing.'

Now, as she remembered that taut exchange, Kristin sighed. Oh yeah, she thought, this was going to be a lot of fun!

There was the scratch of a key in the front door. Kristin sprang to her feet as it opened.

'Anybody home?' Susan called from the foyer.

Kristin took a deep breath. 'I'm in the kitchen, Suze.'

Her room-mate smiled brightly as she came into the room. 'Hi,' she said. 'Umm. Is that fresh coffee I smell?'

'Yes. Help yourself.' Kristin wet her lips as she watched the other girl fill a cup. 'How was your flight?'

'OK, I guess. I mean, what can happen that's exciting between here and Salt Lake City?' Susan sank into a chair and eased off her shoes. 'How about you? Everything all right?'

'Oh, sure. Fine.'

Kristin looked at her room-mate. Susan looked tired this evening. No, not just tired. Worried. Upset.

'Suze? Are you OK?'

Susan smiled brightly. 'Sure.'

Kristin smiled back. The minutes slipped away in silence, and then she cleared her throat.

'Susan, I have to talk to you.'

'Kristin, something's come up.'

The women laughed. 'You first,' Susan said.

Kristin cleared her throat again. 'I've been thinking about what you said. About my boss, I mean. And—and you're right, he does expect too much of me. That's why—that's why——'

Susan interrupted. 'What I really meant was that nobody should get into a rut at work. We all need a change every now and then, don't you think?'

Kristin nodded. 'Yes. And we can't let employers walk all over us.'

'Exactly. It's up to us to do what's best for ourselves. Right?'

'Right. Which is why—it's why...' Kristin paused. 'Suze? How are you fixed financially?'

Her room-mate stared at her. 'What's that got to do with what we were talking about?'

'Nothing. I mean, well—I know we said we'd never borrow from each other, but...'

Susan shrugged. 'Yeah, but that was before we got to be friends. Look, if you're short this week, I can lend you a couple of bucks.'

'No. Well, I—I'm not talking about being short. Not exactly.' Kristin touched her tongue to her lips. 'What

I mean is, well, suppose something came up and—
and . . . I was thinking about the rent, you see, and . . .'

Susan looked at her. 'Me, too,' she said quickly.
'That's just what I was——'

'Because you see, the thing is, I—I . . .' The women's
eyes met. 'You'll never believe what happened,' Kristin
said in a rush. 'Seth Richards—my boss—is being transferred to Rome. And he asked me to go with him.'

Her room-mate stared at her. 'He did what?' she said
softly.

'You heard me. He just—he just . . .' Kristin pushed
back her chair and got to her feet. 'Imagine his nerve,
Suze. He just dropped it on me, without even asking me
if I wanted to go.' She frowned. 'Well, of course, I told
him I had obligations here. I told him——'

'But that's marvellous!' Susan threw her head back
and laughed. 'Thank you, lord,' she said, 'I owe you
one.'

Kristin gaped at her friend. 'What are you talking
about?'

'Miracles,' Susan said happily, 'that's what I'm talking
about!' She scrambled to her feet and grabbed Kristin
in a bear-hug. 'What a sweetheart you are,' she babbled.
'Worrying about me, afraid of what might happen to
me because you weren't going to be here to pay your
half of the rent.'

Bewildered, Kristin shook her head. 'No,' she said
slowly, 'that's not what I meant at all.'

But Susan wasn't listening. 'I feel like a rat,' she said,
drawing back and looking solemnly into Kristin's eyes.
'I mean, I wasn't half as good a person as you. When
Donna Ames called and said she could get me on the
overseas route with her, I just said, "go on, do it!" And
then I walked around wondering how to tell you I might
be leaving, too chicken to face you and say, "Kristin,
can you handle the rent on your own?"'

Kristin stared at her in horror. 'What?'

'And then, when I got the word today that my transfer had come through, I thought, how am I gonna tell this to Kristin?' Susan beamed. 'But here you are, off to Italy, and here I am, off to overseas flights, and to heck with the fancy rent on this place.'

No, Kristin thought, no. This couldn't be happening.

'You mean,' she said slowly, her eyes riveted to Susan's, 'you're giving up your half of the flat?'

Susan grinned. 'What great timing, huh? The landlord can keep this overpriced shanty—and you and I can power up and blast off!' Her grin broadened. 'It's a crazy world, isn't it? Here I was, worried stiff about what would happen—and just look at how well things went. I mean, everything came out just fine!'

Kristin sank into a chair. She wanted to lay her head on the table and weep. Instead, she looked up at her room-mate's smiling face and forced herself to smile in return.

'Yes,' she said softly, 'it certainly did.'

CHAPTER SIX

BY MORNING, Kristin had accepted that she had no alternative but to accept the transfer to Rome. New York was exciting, but it was also unforgiving. In its lexicon of horrors, being jobless and homeless were in a tight race for top honours—and, in the blink of an eye, she would be both.

She took the subway to work. The train was jammed, as always. People swayed against each other as the packed carriage lurched into the station. Bodies brushed against bodies, feet trampled feet, but all these urban survivors had long ago learned to live through the indignities of such close encounters. The key was to avoid eye contact, to put an invisible wall around you and pretend you weren't really where you were.

The door slid open and Kristin stumbled out on to the platform, pushed along by the crowd. She wouldn't have to pretend much longer, she thought suddenly. Soon, she'd be in Italy.

For the first time since the day Seth had sprung the news of his transfer, she felt a faint tug of excitement. Italy—the very name sounded exotic. She'd always longed to travel, but it was expensive. Except for a budget-priced week in Mexico, she'd never been anywhere.

She hurried up the steps from the station to the street. Italy, she thought again, she was going to Italy. To the ancient city of Rome. What could be so awful about that?

Kristin's spirits lifted. Maybe it would all work out, she thought as she pushed open the steel and glass door to the Harbrace building.

'Morning.'

She smiled at the lift starter. 'Good morning.'

'You beat the boss to work today,' he said with a grin.

Kristin's smile faded as the lift doors closed after her. Seth wasn't in yet. Well, that was good news. In all her determination to convince herself that she'd survive her new assignment, she'd somehow forgotten one vital fact.

She would have to tell Seth that she'd go with him.

She took a deep breath as the doors slid open and she stepped out into the corridor. How would she break the news? He'd been so cold and arrogant when she'd refused the Rome assignment. And she—she'd been so damned positive that there were alternatives she could take.

Her heels tapped lightly against the tiled floor as she made her way to the door of her office. Telling him she'd decided to go with him was like admitting defeat. At the very least, it would be humiliating. What would she say to him?

Good morning, Mr Richards, I'm not quitting my job.

Kristin grimaced as she put away her handbag and drew open the vertical blinds beside her desk. She could just imagine his reaction to that. He'd say something cutting and sarcastic, or perhaps he'd just smile smugly— either way, she'd be left with the sour taste that came of eating humble pie.

'Morning, Kristin.'

She jumped and spun towards the door. The secretary from the office across the hall was standing just inside the doorway.

'God, you scared me half to death,' Kristin said with a little laugh.

'How's everything?'

Kristin stared at the girl. 'Fine,' she said. 'Did you—did you want something?'

'No, no. Just thought I'd pop in to say hello.' She glanced past Kristin. 'Boss isn't in yet, huh?'

'No, not yet.'

'Umm. Well, I'll see you later.'

Kristin nodded. What was that all about? she wondered, frowning as she sat down at her desk. In the months she'd worked here, the two of them had never exchanged more than a dozen words, and now, all of a sudden, here she was, all smiles and . . .

Wait a minute. Had the rumour mill started grinding—was the jockeying for her job under way already? Yes, of course, why wouldn't it be? Days had passed since she'd told Seth she didn't want the Rome assignment.

Kristin sagged back in the chair. How could she have been so stupid? He wouldn't have waited forever to replace her. He'd probably already given the go-ahead to Mrs Dowd. For all she knew, her replacement might, even now, be standing in the lift.

Kristin's mouth went dry. She needed this job, damn it, she couldn't afford to let it get away from her. Quickly, she reached for the phone. She'd call Mrs Dowd, she'd tell her . . .

The light was blinking on the answering machine. How had she missed it? she thought, depressing the button.

To her surprise, Seth's curt voice filled the room.

'Miss Marshall. I won't be in for the next couple of days. I'm leaving for the Philadelphia office this morning. If you need me, I'll be there until late afternoon. I'll be in Kansas City tonight and tomorrow, and the St Louis office after that. I'll be back some time Thursday.'

There was a pause and she reached out to shut off the machine, just as Seth spoke again.

'Please speak with Mrs Dowd about setting up interviews with the applicants she's screened to replace you.'

There was another silence; when Seth's voice resumed, it had turned gruff. 'I'm sorry you won't be going with me, Kristin.'

The tape beeped twice as it reached the end of the message and the line went dead.

Kristin closed her eyes and put her hands to her temples. Too late, she thought, it was too late to talk to him and tell him she'd changed her mind. She'd lost her job. She'd lost more than that; God, she'd lost—she'd lost...

'Miss Marshall?'

Her eyes flew open. Mrs Dowd stood in the open doorway, watching her. Kristin swallowed drily and rose to her feet.

'Good morning, Mrs Dowd. I was just going to call you.'

The head of Personnel nodded. 'Yes, I thought you might. When does Mr Richards want to start his interviews?'

'I—I haven't checked his calendar yet,' she said slowly.

'I was hoping to begin day after tomorrow, Miss Marshall. We really have very little time.'

Kristin drew in her breath. 'I told you, I haven't looked at his schedule.'

'Perhaps I should speak with Mr Richards directly.'

Kristin's eyes met the older woman's. 'I'm Mr Richards' secretary,' she said carefully. 'It's my job to——'

'Well, it won't be your job much longer, will it?' Mrs Dowd smiled coolly. 'I already have three applicants for the position. Not everyone views an overseas assignment as a hardship.'

'I didn't view it as a hardship. It was just...' Kristin cleared her throat. 'Anyway, there's been a change of plans,' she said briskly. 'I've decided to accept the transfer after all.'

Mrs Dowd's brows rose. 'Really.' It was not a question, and Kristin was not foolish enough to respond. After a moment, she shrugged her shoulders. 'Well, I'm afraid you'll have to take that up with Mr Richards.'

'Yes, but you're in charge of hiring. That's why——'

'I can't stop the selection process on your say-so, Miss Marshall. I'll have to see a directive from Mr Richards himself.'

Kristin nodded. It was no more than she might have expected.

'Of course.'

'Talk to him about it as soon as possible, please. I've already invested a good deal of my time in this. I certainly don't want to waste any more.'

'I will,' Kristin promised.

The day passed, and the next. But she couldn't talk to Seth, not over the telephone. His calls to the office were brief, almost curt.

'Any messages? Anything on my desk that can't wait until I get back?'

There would be a quick exchange of information, and then the conversation would end abruptly.

She had no choice; she'd have to wait until Thursday to tell him she'd changed her mind. Meanwhile, the news that she'd turned down the Rome transfer had spread through the building like wildfire. Everyone wanted to tell her how crazy she was—and several wanted to let her know they'd offered to take her place.

'Dowd asked for applicants for the slot. You don't mind, do you, Kristin?' they said.

She shook her head. 'No,' she said each time, 'I don't mind.'

What else could she do, until she spoke with Seth?

By Wednesday morning she was fielding indignant calls from Mrs Dowd, who was demanding to know if Seth had decided whether or not to proceed with the interviews. Kristin danced around the issue, carefully avoiding an answer.

'I really must have his decision, Miss Marshall.'

Kristin closed her eyes. 'All right,' she said. 'I promise you, I'll get things straightened out today.'

She glanced at the clock as she hung up the phone. Seth would be in St Louis now. If his meetings went off as scheduled, he'd be phoning soon. Somehow, she'd get up her courage and tell him she'd had a change of heart before he could hang up.

But he didn't call. Kristin kept waiting for the phone to ring, but it was silent. She pounded away at the typewriter, glancing at the clock as the minutes flew by with maddening disregard for her predicament, and then, as suddenly as ever, the ribbon snapped.

Kristin slammed her hand against the keyboard, noting with grim satisfaction the sudden jam of print that appeared on the letter she'd been typing, and then she shut off the machine and took off the cover.

'Damn,' she said between her teeth as she bent over it. Seconds later, she looked up in triumph, the old ribbon cartridge clutched in her hand.

'That's it,' she said. 'That's what happens when you don't fight me.'

'That's always good advice.'

The hair rose on the nape of her neck. She turned quickly, knowing even before she saw Seth that he'd been standing in the open doorway, watching her, and knowing too, with a rush of bitter-sweet pleasure, that she had never been as happy to see anyone in her life as she was to see him.

Kristin struggled to get herself together. He'd taken her completely by surprise, of course; he wasn't due until tomorrow, but the shock she felt, the sudden gallop of her heart, wasn't only the result of seeing him standing there with just a hint of a smile curving over his lips as if he'd waited all day just for this moment. Her breath caught. She had missed him, she had missed him terribly, and the sudden realisation terrified her.

It took all her strength to speak calmly.

'I didn't expect you back today,' she said. 'You said you'd be in tomorrow...'

Her words trailed off into silence. Seth smiled and leaned away from the wall.

'I wound up my business sooner than I expected,' he said. 'How are things going on this end?' His smile broadened. 'Aside from the typewriter wars, I mean.'

His smile was so genuine that she relaxed a little. 'I won the latest skirmish,' she said, holding up the dead cartridge.

Seth's teeth flashed a quick grin. 'So I see. No other problems, though?'

'No,' she answered, and then she swallowed drily. 'Except—except there's something I should discuss with you.'

His smile faded. 'Yes, all right.' She watched as he reached down and picked up his bag. 'In my office, please.'

His tone was still pleasant. But the look on his face made her spirits tumble.

He knew she wanted the job, Kristin thought suddenly. And he had already arranged for someone to take her place. She was sure of it.

She followed after him slowly and paused in the doorway, watching as he leafed through the letters stacked on his desk.

God, how she hated Mrs Dowd. And she hated the unknown girl who would go to Italy in her place, hated herself for having been so foolish as to have turned the job down in the first place.

She'd have to start the struggle to find a new flat first thing tomorrow. And on Sunday she'd have to read the employment ads from end to end again.

Suddenly, she couldn't seem to breathe. Who was she kidding? She would find a place to live and a job, and if they weren't as good as what she had now, what would it matter? Seth would be gone, he'd be thousands of miles from here, and she'd never see him again. That was what this was all about.

She'd been right to turn down the transfer. She couldn't go to Italy with Seth. It was too dangerous. It was...

A little sound burst from her throat and Seth looked up and stared at her.

'Did you say something, Kristin?'

She shook her head. 'No,' she said quickly. Their eyes met and she looked down at the floor. 'I'm sorry,' she said, 'I forgot my notepad. Let me just...'

Seth unbuttoned his jacket and perched on the edge of his desk. 'You said there was something you wanted to discuss.'

His eyes were on her face, but they were hooded and impenetrable. Her teeth closed lightly over her bottom lip and she bit down until she felt a faint lick of pain.

'Did I?' she said at last. Her voice sounded puzzled. 'I'm sorry, but I can't... The Thompson memo,' she said when his eyebrows rose, 'that was it. I'll just——'

'Sit down, Kristin.'

His voice was soft, but it commanded. She moved slowly to the chair opposite his desk and sat—back straight, knees together, fingers laced tightly in her lap, holding herself in place as if she might otherwise shatter into a million pieces.

'Yes, sir,' she said.

Seth smiled. 'I thought we left that behind days ago. My name is Seth, remember?'

Seth. Well, she could call him that safely now. In just a little while, he'd be gone.

'Seth,' she said politely, 'Mr Thompson asked...'

She fell silent as he looked at her. Why was he watching her that way? There was a question in his eyes; she felt as if—as if he was measuring her and the moment.

Get to it, she thought desperately, and the words that had to be said tumbled from her mouth in a breathless rush.

'Mrs Dowd's lined up some applicants for you to interview. She wants to know when you want to begin.'

'Why would I go through all that nonsense, Kristin?'

'Well, I know you're pressed for time. But——'

'And why would I lie to those young women?'

She stared at him. 'Lie to them?'

He got to his feet and walked to the window, his hands tucked into the pockets of his trousers.

'I'd have to pretend I was considering them for the assignment.' He turned slowly towards her. 'And all the while I'd know that you'd already accepted it.'

A silence fell over the room. Kristin waited for him to say something more, but he simply stood there and watched her. Finally, she moistened her lips with the tip of her tongue.

'How did you...?'

A smiled tugged at the corners of his mouth. 'The rumour mill,' he said softly. 'It works on executive levels, too.'

She let out her breath. 'I—I wanted to tell you myself. To discuss it, I mean.'

His eyes moved over her face, lingering for a heartbeat on her lips.

'When did you change your mind?'

'The other day. But——'

'Why?'

She stared at him. 'Why?'

'Yes. Why did you decide to go with me?'

Kristin shrugged her shoulders. 'It's—it's complicated,' she said. 'I'm not sure you'd——'

Seth smiled. 'Try me.'

Her chin lifted. 'I couldn't get another job as good as this one,' she said, her eyes meeting his. 'You were quite right about that.' She waited for a quick bit of sarcasm, but none came. 'And—and there were other factors.'

'Such as?'

What did he want her to say? He seemed to be waiting for some special admission, some acknowledgement only he understood.

'I don't see what this——'

'A few days ago,' he said, his voice suddenly cool, 'you acted as if going with me to Rome was one step removed from a trip to hell. Then, all of a sudden, you damned near begged Betty Dowd to——'

Kristin flushed. 'I didn't beg.'

'I don't think it's unreasonable for me to ask what changed your mind, do you, Kristin?'

Her head rose. 'I told you. There was no other job available. And my share of the rent——'

'Your share?' Seth's voice became a hiss. 'What do you mean, your share?'

She tossed her head. 'A place to live isn't cheap in this city, you know. The rent's very high. And when my room-mate decided to leave...'

His eyes turned to ice, and Kristin put her hand to her mouth. What had she said? He thought she had a live-in lover; how could she have forgotten?

'Leave,' he repeated softly, in tones even colder than his eyes. 'He left you, just like that?'

Kristin got to her feet. 'Look,' she said in a voice that quavered, 'I don't really think——'

'What kind of son of a bitch is this man anyway?'

'You don't know the whole story. You can't judge——'

Seth let out his breath. 'No,' he said sharply, 'no, I suppose I can't.' He turned away and ran his hand through his hair. When he faced her again, his expression was grim but he had himself under control. 'Why didn't you tell me you'd changed your mind when I phoned?'

Kristin shrugged her shoulders. 'I would have. But there never seemed to be time.'

'I might have made other arrangements,' he said, his voice flat.

Kristin felt a sudden constriction in her chest. 'Have you?' she asked in a papery whisper. 'Made other arrangements, I mean?'

Seth stared at her.

'No,' he said finally. 'I haven't.'

Her heart leaped against her ribs. 'I'm glad,' she said before she could think. 'I'm so...'

She stumbled into silence. But it was too late; the words seemed to hang between them, vibrating in the still air.

He took a step forward and her heart stopped beating. But he stopped when he was still at arm's length and, after what seemed an eternity, he smiled.

'I didn't want anyone but you, Kristin,' he said softly. 'Don't you know that? I just kept hoping you'd change your mind and say you'd go with me.'

Later, after her life lay in pieces around her, Kristin would look back and remember this moment with painful clarity. The slow lift of Seth's head as his eyes sought hers, the caress of his voice, the electric stillness in the air—she would remember all of it and realise what a fool she'd been not to have known what lay ahead.

But just then it was hard enough to draw breath into her lungs, let alone think coherent thoughts. The room, the whole world, seemed to be spinning away, and suddenly she was trembling, her heart pounding as if it were trying to leap free of her chest.

Look away from him, she thought desperately, and finally, although it took all her strength, she did.

The world titled back to its axis, and sanity returned.

'Yes,' she said calmly. 'I realise that this was a wonderful opportunity. A few months abroad will look good on my resumé.'

Seth let out his breath. 'Yes,' he said, just as calmly, 'I'm sure it will.' He gave her the same polite, meaningless smile he had given her many times before. 'Not that my motives are all that altruistic. You know me, you know my habits. Things will go far more smoothly for me than if I had to set up in Rome with someone new at my side.' He sat down behind his desk. 'Have you a passport?'

'Yes. I went to Mexico on vacation last year—you don't really need a passport, but the travel agent said it would simplify things, so I got one.'

He nodded. 'Good,' he said briskly. 'The company will arrange for your visa—you'll need one to work overseas.' He glanced at his watch and frowned. 'Now, if you don't mind, I'd like to get some letters out. My successor's going to have enough to do without cleaning up after me.'

Kristin rose to her feet. 'I'll get my notepad.'

'Fine. Oh—before you come in, you'd better call Accounting. You want to be sure they know your salary cheque should be mailed to the Rome office.'

She nodded. It was going to be easy, she thought with relief. Whatever foolishness had gone on was over. It had been her fantasy anyway, not his. She had read things into the way he'd looked at her minutes ago. And what he'd said—about wanting only her—was what any smugly satisfied employer would say when his secretary demonstrated her loyalty.

Seth would treat her just as he had before, courteously and impersonally. And she—well, she could hold up her end. She was doing that now, wasn't she? She was back to being the perfect secretary.

'Thanks for reminding me,' she said. 'I'll call Mrs Dowd, too, and tell her not to bother with any more applicants—if that's all right with you.'

'Fine,' he said. She had her hand on the doorknob when he said her name. 'Kristin?'

She turned to him, a polite smile on her face. But the smile slipped when she saw the way he was looking at her.

'He's a fool,' he said softly. 'Your lover's a fool. Any man who'd leave you has to be.'

Then he bent his head over the letters on his desk. After a long, long time, Kristin stepped out of his office and closed the door quietly behind her. But it seemed to take forever until she stopped trembling.

CHAPTER SEVEN

YOUR lover's a fool, he'd said. Any man who'd leave you has to be.

Kristin couldn't get the softly spoken words out of her head. What had Seth really meant? Had he been talking to her as a man talked to a woman—or had it been just another way of saying you're a damned good secretary, Miss Marshall, you're worth your weight in gold?

Lavish, meaningless praise wasn't unusual in her world. Girls in the steno pool giggled about old Mr Belkin, who called his typists 'treasures' and 'fair flowers of womanhood'.

And the head of Sales, Mr Devers—Kristin had filled in for his ailing secretary for almost a month last year. What was it he'd said the time he'd introduced her to his wife?

'Here's Kristin, the only other beautiful woman who understands me.'

Girls on the receiving end of all that empty talk were supposed to smile and blush prettily—and they always did, except when they were alone.

'Save the compliments and give me a raise in pay,' the more cynical among them would mutter over tuna-fish sandwiches in the lunch-room.

And someone who'd been in the steno pool longer would make a face and respond.

'It's cheaper to raise the compliments and save the pay,' she'd say, and everyone would laugh.

Well, then, Seth's comment fell into the same category. It had just been an empty bit of nonsense, a throw-away line that had about as much meaning as gold stars given out in nursery school.

That was right—wasn't it?

Kristin told herself that until she believed it—and then she'd remember the softness in his voice, the way it had caressed her, and her heart would turn over in her breast.

She didn't know what to believe. Worse still, she didn't know what she *wanted* to believe—and that scared the life out of her.

Work became her salvation. There were a thousand and one things to do, and hardly enough time in which to do them. It was simple to fill her waking hours to the brim and end up tumbling into bed each night in a state of mindless exhaustion.

She started by clearing out her desk and files at the office. She had to take on Seth's desk, as well—he was off on a whirlwind round of meetings and briefings.

There were few personal items on his desk: a handful of news clippings that related to his career, a news magazine with an article in it about Harbrace, and a silver-framed photograph of a smiling family, the father with his arm around his son, the mother holding a baby in her arms. The clothing and hair styles were twenty years or so out of date. She knew instinctively it was a photo of Seth and his family: she could see the man hidden in the boy's childish features, and she smiled before wrapping the picture and tucking it into a box labelled with Seth's name.

When he phoned and said he'd be out the rest of the week, she breathed a sigh of relief. That meant she wouldn't see him again until they met at the airport the evening of their departure—and perhaps not even then, if she was lucky. She and Seth were booked to Rome on the same flight. But they would not be in the same cabin.

Mrs Dowd seemed to take a special pleasure in telling her that. 'Here are your tickets,' she said officiously. 'You'll be in economy.' The head of Personnel paused, a tight little smile on her pursed lips. 'Mr Richards will fly first class, of course.'

If she expected Kristin to balk, she was mistaken.

Kristin smiled back. 'Of course,' she said politely.

The snub, if that was what it was, was most welcome. She had not looked forward to spending six hours in the narrow confines of a plane with Seth.

'And this is the key to the flat Harbrace has rented for you.' Mrs Dowd handed her a small envelope. 'The address is inside.'

'Thank you.' Kristin hesitated. 'Is it—where is the flat located, do you know?'

'Near the Piazza Navona, I believe.' Mrs Dowd peered at her over her glasses. 'Why? Do you know Rome, Miss Marshall?'

Kristin shook her head. 'No,' she said quickly, 'I just— I've been doing some reading, and I wondered...'

She let her words trail into silence. What she'd wondered was if she'd be living anywhere near her boss, but how could she ask such a question?

She could only hope their flats would be on opposite sides of the city.

When she finished sorting things out at work, she barely took a breath before tackling the bigger job waiting at her apartment.

Everything she owned had to be gone through and sorted: this would go with her to Italy, this would be given away, this would be placed in storage, courtesy of Harbrace.

That she had accumulated so many things in the five years she'd lived in New York surprised her. The flat had come furnished, and somehow Kristin had never imagined that she'd added all that much that was personal to it.

But she had. A coffee-maker. A toaster. Mugs. A china teapot. Books. A tape player, and stacks of tapes to go with it. There was even a bag of yarn she'd rescued after one of the other tenants had tossed it out.

'I'm going to knit a sweater,' she'd said when Susan eyed the bits and pieces of wool with a dubious eye.

She hadn't, of course. And now here she was, staring at the untouched yarn months later.

Susan laughed as she stepped into Kristin's bedroom.

'At least that's an easy decision,' she said. 'Send it back where it came from. I can hear the incinerator calling.'

Kristin looked up. 'How're you doing?'

Her room-mate shrugged. 'Not too badly. I've got a stack of things for the charity outlet shop—just one more closet to go, and I'll be done. How about you?'

'I'm getting there. It's easier this time than the last.'

'When you moved in here, you mean?'

Kristin shook her head. 'That wasn't anything. I only had to go across town.' She sank back on her heels. 'What I was remembering was packing up and coming here, to the city.'

'Ah. The great trek East, you mean. Yeah, that must have been something.'

Kristin nodded. 'It was,' she said, remembering how the pain of what was driving her to New York had eclipsed everything else. In the end, her mother had packed for her, assuring her that whatever things she left behind would be safe until she wanted them.

She looked at Susan and smiled. 'There's no attic for the overflow this time,' she said, and she shoved the bag of yarn against the wall. 'Out with it,' she said firmly.

Her friend grinned. 'That's the spirit. Once you get the hang of this, it's not so bad.' She sank down on the floor next to Kristin. 'What about all that?' she asked, nodding at the stacks of tapes and books. 'Are you leaving that stuff behind?'

Kristin pushed her hair out of her eyes. 'Most of it. If you see anything you want, it's yours with my blessing.'

Susan leaned forward. 'Strauss waltzes,' she said, making a face. 'Thanks, but no thanks. But I'll take this,' she said, plucking out a Bob Dylan tape. 'Oh, and definitely this,' she added, laying claim to an old Beatles album. She grinned. 'When I was twelve, I'd have sold my soul for tapes like these.'

Kristin laughed. 'You're kidding.'

'Nope.' She leaned over and plucked at another tape. 'My father wouldn't let me bring rock and roll albums into the house.' She grinned. 'I think his theory was that anything you want that badly can't be good for you.'

Like Seth, Kristin thought immediately. A sharp pain knifed just below her heart. Quickly, she pushed the box of tapes aside and got to her feet.

'Maybe your father was right,' she said.

Susan looked up. 'Hey,' she said, 'what's wrong? Did I say something I shouldn't?'

Kristin managed a smile. 'Forget the tapes, Suze,' she said, throwing open the door to her wardrobe. 'Give me a hand with the really hard part. What clothing shall I take and what shall I leave?'

'Take it all,' her room-mate said without hesitation.

'Don't be silly. The baggage restrictions...'

The other woman grinned. 'What restrictions? Harbrace will pay for any excess.'

'Well, yes. But...'

'You never know what you'll need, that's my motto.'

'Not this,' Kristin said, pulling a pair of cotton trousers from a hanger. 'Or this,' she added, nodding to a short-sleeved silk shirt. 'It's autumn, after all.'

'Rome's supposed to be warm this time of year. You'll be right near the Mediterranean, remember?'

Kristin sighed. 'Well, I certainly won't need anything like this,' she said, lifting out a short black crêpe de Chine dress. Sequins were scattered across the bodice, glinting in the light like tiny suns blazing against a night sky.

Susan cocked her head to the side. 'Umm, that's yummy. Where's it been hiding?'

'I bought it last year, for the Christmas party. But I never got around to wearing it.'

'You never got around to letting me get my paws on it, you mean.' Susan smiled. 'Have a heart—the poor thing needs an airing. Give it to me and I'll see to its welfare.'

Kristin laughed. 'Take it,' she said, holding the dress out to her friend. 'I haven't been very good to it, that's for sure.'

'No, don't be silly. I can't take something so pricey from you. I was just joking.'

'Well, I wasn't. It's much too dressy—I shouldn't have bought it in the first place. I'll never wear it.'

Susan grinned. 'Have a little faith, friend. What will you put on if some gorgeous count invites you to dine at his *palazzo*?'

'Somehow, I don't think that's going to be one of my problems,' Kristin said, smiling at her friend in return.

'Well, it might be. Rome's probably full of tall, dark, and handsome men. How do you know you won't meet one?'

But I already have, Kristin thought, right here in New York. Her breath caught in her throat. God, what was happening to her? What was...?

'Kristin? Are you OK?'

She swallowed drily. 'Yes,' she said, 'I'm fine. I'm just—I'm just tired, I guess, from dragging all these boxes around.'

'Yeah. Me, too.' Susan rose to her feet and dusted off her jeans. 'Tell you what—why don't I make us some tea?'

Kristin nodded. 'That sounds good. Just give me a minute.'

'The dress,' Susan said. Kristin looked at her. 'The little black dress you're going to consign to the discard heap—go on, take it along.' She smiled. 'What have you got to lose? You might just meet up with that count after all.'

'You're just an old romantic,' Kristin said, smiling a little. 'Go on, start the tea. I'll be right in.'

She looked at the dress as her friend hurried from the room. It was foolish to toss it out, wasn't it? And it certainly wouldn't take up much room in her luggage.

Kristin sighed. Susan was right, she had nothing to lose—and everything to gain. Maybe there *was* a handsome Roman in her future, one who would drive all these insane thoughts about Seth from her mind, once and for all.

'Next stop, Italy,' she whispered, and she added the black dress to the pile of clothing stacked on the bed.

As luck would have it, she and Susan were both leaving New York within hours of each other. Departure Day, her room-mate called it, shortening the phrase to D-Day without so much as an apologetic shrug to history.

'I'll miss you,' she said tearfully as she gave Kristin a goodbye hug late that last morning.

Kristin hugged her back. 'Me, too,' she said.

'I'll telephone before my plane takes off, if there's time.'

The flat seemed terribly empty after Susan left. Kristin kept glancing at her watch, wishing away the hours until her own departure. She was just stepping from the shower when the phone rang. Quickly, she slipped into her robe and raced down the hall to her bedroom.

Susan, she thought, smiling, and she snatched up the phone.

'Hi,' she said breathlessly. 'I know it sounds silly, but I miss you already. I was hoping you'd call.'

There was a silence, and then the sound of a man's dry, somewhat curt voice.

'I'm sorry to disappoint you, Kristin. It's not who you think it is.'

She could barely get his name out. 'Seth?'

'Yes.' His voice was hard. 'It's only me.'

Her throat closed. Seth had never called her at home before. It put her off balance, somehow. There was something disconcerting about talking to him as she sat on the edge of her rumpled bed, dressed only in a thin silk robe.

She rose to her feet, gathered the trailing cord in her hand and walked into the hallway.

'Yes?' she said cautiously. Her heart was hammering, and that was silly. There was no reason to be nervous.

'Look, if this is a bad time to call...'

'No,' she said quickly, 'no, it isn't. I'm just surprised to...' She cleared her throat. 'Is something wrong?'

He hesitated, and then she heard the breath sigh from his lungs.

'Yes,' he said. 'There's been a change in plans.'

Her heart sank like a lead weight. She wasn't going with him. Mrs Dowd had convinced him to take someone else, or he'd thought it over and decided it was unwise. Yes, that was it. And he was probably right—it *was* unwise, she knew that in her bones.

'I was going to—to make a stop before going to the airport. But I've changed my mind. So I thought—I wondered if you'd like my taxi to pick you up.'

Kristin let out her breath. 'Go to the airport together, you mean?'

'Yes. I could be there in...'

She closed her eyes, envisaging them riding to the airport together as if they were setting out on a holiday.

But they weren't. They were employer and employee. She had to remember that.

'Kristin?'

She swallowed drily. 'Thanks,' she said, 'but I've——'

'You needn't explain.' Seth's voice was flat. 'Well, then, I'll see you on the plane.'

No, she thought, closing her eyes, he wouldn't. Thank God for that much.

But before she could say anything more, Seth hung up.

The flight was going to be endless—Kristin was sure of that within minutes of being airborne. She had the middle seat in the middle aisle of the big 747—was that a special touch of Mrs Dowd's? she wondered. The man to her right kept oozing over the arm rest that separated them. The woman to her left was reading the *New York Times*, and the pages were half draped across Kristin's lap.

There wasn't any sense in asking for another seat. The plane was jammed. The best she could hope for was——

'What are you doing back here?'

The harsh, familiar voice made her jump. She looked up, straight into Seth's angry eyes.

'What do you mean, what am I doing here?' she said foolishly. 'This is my seat.'

'In economy class?' he said, spitting out the words with as much distaste as if he'd found her in a leper colony.

Kristin glanced around her. Both her seat-mates were watching her, listening to the strange conversation without any attempt at pretending otherwise.

'My ticket's for here,' she said in a low voice. 'Seth, I wish you'd——'

'Get your things.'

She stared at him. 'Don't be ridiculous. I can't just change...'

But he wasn't paying attention to her protests. 'Are your things in here?' he demanded, pointing at the overhead storage compartment.

'Yes. But...'

He opened it and lifted out her leather bag, then nodded at the magazine tucked into the seat pocket in front of her.

'And this? Is it yours?'

'Yes,' she said again. 'But I can't——'

'You can and you shall.' His hand closed around her elbow, the fingers pressing hard into her skin. Kristin rose from her seat, her face flushing as she caught the stares of the passengers seated nearby.

'Seth,' she whispered, 'really, you can't do this. They won't let you.'

But he was already doing it, taking her the length of the cabin while a smiling flight attendant led the way. Another attendant pulled aside the curtain that separated economy from first class.

'Nice to have you with us, Miss Marshall,' she said.

Seth propelled her to a seat near the front of the plane.

'Sit,' he ordered when she opened her mouth to protest.

Kristin glanced around her. The cabin was half empty. The other passengers were doing their best to pretend uninterest, but she could sense that all ears were tuned in her direction. She slipped into the seat, then glared at Seth as he sat down beside her.

'Would you mind telling me what all this is about?' she hissed.

'Why did you ticket yourself in economy?'

'It's not a crime, is it?'

'I asked you a question, Kristin. Please answer it.'

She sighed. 'I didn't. Mrs Dowd made the arrangements.'

Seth nodded. 'Yes,' he said grimly, 'I should have expected as much.'

'Look, this is ridiculous.' Kristin put her hands on the arm rests of her chair and began to rise to her feet. 'My ticket's not for first class.'

Seth's hand clamped around her wrist like a manacle.

'You're staying here,' he said.

'But why?'

His eyes swept over her face. 'Is being with me so distasteful?'

'No, of course not.'

'Don't you want to be with me, Kristin?'

Her breath caught. His eyes were like hot coals in his face, and suddenly the simple question was one she dared not answer.

'I told you, I don't belong in this compartment. My ticket——'

'You belong with me,' he said sharply. 'You're my secretary. When we travel for business, we travel together. Surely you can see the logic in that.'

Kristin stared at him. Of course there was logic to what he'd said. Seth usually travelled with a tape recorder, but this time he had her along. She could take notes or dictation or...

'Kristin? Do you understand?'

She nodded. 'Yes.'

A muscle twitched in Seth's jaw. 'I hope so.' He watched her for a moment, and then he put his head back. 'Why don't you try and get some sleep?' he said, as if nothing out of the ordinary had happened. 'We've a long flight ahead of us.'

Out of the corner of her eye, Kristin saw him stretch out his legs and ease his seat back. Finally, after what seemed a long time, he closed his eyes.

Silence settled over the cabin. Kristin shifted in her seat. It *was* more comfortable here. Seth was right. It was logical that she be beside him. She was his secretary. Being near at hand was part of her job. It was what she was paid to do.

Her lashes fluttered to her cheeks. She was exhausted. The last days had been draining; she couldn't think straight. She couldn't...

Suddenly, her eyes flew open. A question as corrosive as bile rose within her.

Was she sitting in the seat that should have been Jeanne Lester's?

A dark wave of some indefinable emotion beat through her. What did it matter? Jeanne wasn't here. *She* was. It was she who would be at Seth's side in Rome, she who would share his days, she who would...

Kristin bit down on her lip. Enough, she told herself. Her mind was spinning. It was time to stop thinking for a while.

She closed her eyes again and gave herself over to the hypnotic drone of the engines. After a little while, she slept, and, as she should have known it would, the dream came to claim her...

She was walking through a garden. Flowers bloomed everywhere; she could hear the sound of water falling over stones, splashing and tumbling to earth.

The garden was lovely. But she was alone. And she didn't want to be alone. She wanted—she wanted...

'Kristin.'

A smile curved across her lips. It was his voice. He was here, he'd come for her again. It had been so long.

'Kristin.'

His breath whispered against her hair as she went into his arms.

'You came back,' she sighed, and he smiled.

'Did you think I wouldn't?' His arms tightened around her. 'I want you beside me, Kristin.'

'*Kristin*...'

'Kristin?'

The whisper penetrated her dream. Kristin's eyes flew open, then widened with shock. She was lying in the warm curve of Seth's arm. Her head was cradled against his shoulder; her mouth was almost against his throat. The heat of his body blazed against hers.

Colour flamed in her cheeks. 'I'm sorry,' she said as she pulled free of his encircling arm. 'I—I must have fallen asleep.'

'You were dreaming,' Seth said softly.

His voice was low and intimate. For one terrible moment, her heart seemed to stop beating.

'Did I—did I say anything?'

He smiled. 'No. But it seemed to be a pretty good dream. I hated to wake you.'

Kristin put her hands to her face. Her cheeks felt as if they were on fire. Wisps of hair had escaped the neat knot at the back of her head; she smoothed them back, then touched her fingers to the Peter Pan collar of her white silk blouse.

She felt as if she were coming undone, as if she needed to reassure herself that she was still the same person she'd always been.

'I'm sorry if I disturbed you,' she said carefully.

He stretched lazily, the movements catlike in their economy and grace.

'I caught some sleep, too,' he said. His smile faded, and suddenly she realised how tired he looked. 'The last few days have been pretty hectic.'

Kristin nodded. 'Things have been upside-down at the office, haven't they?'

Seth's mouth twisted. 'And elsewhere. This sudden transfer played havoc with a lot of things.'

Of course. He must have had half a dozen women to say goodbye to. She'd only had to phone her parents and wish Susan well. She hadn't even bothered calling Paul; she'd put him off so many times after the night she'd broken their date that he'd stopped telephoning.

'You must be exhausted,' she said, hating the stiff, prim sound of her words.

But Seth didn't seem to notice. He smiled and looked at her.

'I am. But just the thought of seeing Rome again gives me a second wind.' His smile broadened. 'It's a wonderful city, Kristin. You're going to love it.'

His smile was infectious, and after a moment she smiled back.

'I'm sure I will.' She swivelled towards the window, peering into the clouds as if the city were going to materialise at any second. 'I can hardly believe it,' she said softly. 'A little while ago, I was in New York...'

'About to be smothered by that guy in the window seat or gift-wrapped in newsprint by the lady on the aisle.'

Kristin laughed. 'It's true,' she admitted. 'I don't think I'll ever see a tinned sardine without feeling a twinge of compassion.'

'But you weren't talking about that, were you?'

She shook her head. 'No. I was talking about this,' she said, gesturing towards the window. 'About the fact that I'm really on my way to Italy. I mean, I've never been anywhere before.'

'You've been to Mexico.'

She looked at him in surprise. 'Yes. How did you know?'

'You told me, remember? When I asked if you had a passport, you said you'd got one last year before you vacationed in Mexico.'

Yes, she remembered now. But it surprised her that he remembered; it had been such a meaningless little bit of information, and he'd been so busy with so many things.

'Did you go alone?'

There was a sudden edge to his voice. She glanced at him, puzzled. He was smiling pleasantly, the way people did when they were making small talk. But there was a glittering coolness in his eyes.

'No,' she said. The coldness became ice. 'Well, not exactly. I was in a tour group—but I didn't know anyone.'

Seth let out his breath. 'You *were* alone, then.'

Kristin nodded. 'Yes. I——'

She broke off in confusion. Her lover. Her imaginary lover. Had he thought . . . ?

'Excuse me, Mr Richards.' The flight attendant smiled down at Seth. 'We'll be serving dinner in a little while. Have you had time to make your selection from the menu?'

Seth nodded. 'Yes. But Miss Marshall may wish to...'

Kristin shook her head. How would she look at a menu and make sense out of it? How would she keep it from trembling in her hands?

'That's all right,' she said. She gave Seth a quick smile. 'Whatever you choose is fine with me.'

Hie eyes met hers. 'Is it?'

'Yes. Anything you want.'

'I know exactly what I want, Kristin.'

Seth's gaze moved over her face, heating it until she felt her skin bloom with warmth. She wanted to look away from him, but his eyes caught hers, and she was suddenly powerless to move.

The moment stretched into infinity, and finally the flight attendant cleared her throat.

'Which shall it be, Miss Marshall?' she asked briskly. '*Osso buco? Scaloppine al limone?* Prime ribs, perhaps?'

'Excuse me,' Kristin said in a shaky whisper. She rose and moved past Seth, past the flight attendant, then stepped quickly into the aisle.

'I know exactly what I want,' he'd said.

God help her, so did she.

CHAPTER EIGHT

LEONARDO DA VINCI AIRPORT was a confusion of noise and people. Kristin and Seth moved slowly through Customs and then to the baggage area. At the exit gate, he put his hand on her arm and paused, frowning as he scanned the crowd beyond.

'Harbrace was supposed to send someone to meet us,' he said. 'I would have thought...'

'Signore Richards?' A young man rushed up to them, panting a little and smiling apologetically. 'You *are* Seth Richards, are you not?' he asked with a faint Italian accent.

Seth nodded. 'And you are...?'

'Marco Valenti.' He held out his hand. 'I'm terribly sorry, sir. The traffic was especially heavy today, and I——'

'That's all right, Valenti. Let's just get started, shall we? I'd like to get settled in as soon as possible.'

But Marco Valenti wasn't listening. He was looking at Kristin and smiling.

'*Buon giorno,*' he said. 'You must be Kristin Marshall.'

Kristin smiled back. 'Yes. It's nice to meet you, Mr Valenti.'

'It's Marco, please. Welcome to Rome, Kristin.'

'Valenti.' Seth's voice was crisp. Marco turned quickly to him. 'How far is it into the city?'

'It is not a matter of distance, sir, but of speed.' Marco looked back at Kristin. 'Rome has terrible traffic problems' he said in a pleasant, conversational tone. 'If you think New York is difficult——'

'In that case,' Seth said brusquely, 'I suggest we get moving. See to the luggage, would you, please?'

His hand closed around Kristin's elbow. She had no choice but to match his quick footsteps as he marched past Marco Valenti and out the door.

Kristin's first glimpse of Rome was exciting. Her imagination had fashioned an impossible image of romantic marble ruins beside the Tiber. What awaited her instead was a busy modern city. The roads and streets were, as Marco had warned, a snarl of cars, trucks, and more motorcycles than she'd ever seen before.

Marco had put her into the front passenger seat of his Mercedes. 'Unfortunately, the car is Harbrace's, not mine,' he'd said with a disarming grin. 'I am sure you'll be more comfortable in the rear, sir,' he assured Seth.

As they drove, Marco offered a running commentary on the sights. Seth didn't respond, but Kristin did, with questions and exclamations of delight. After a while, Marco peppered his remarks with little asides directed at her. She laughed when he showed her a mother, father, and two toddlers riding on a passing motorcycle, and nodded eagerly when he pointed to a stand of ancient white pillars set almost casually in the midst of the congested urban landscape.

When they stopped at a red light, Kristin shook her head in disbelief. Despite the stop light, cars crept forward towards the intersection, engines rumbling impatiently, while pedestrians crossed the street without so much as a sideways glance.

Marco glanced over at her. 'It looks impossible, no?' he asked cheerfully.

Kristin laughed. 'It looks impossible, yes. And dangerous. I keep expecting to see bodies strewn all over the streets. How do you make it through in one piece?'

He grinned. 'Ah. You have to learn to think as a Roman.'

'Meaning?'

'Meaning you act as if it were you who owned the road. You just look straight ahead and——'

'The traffic's moving, Valenti.' Seth's voice echoed coldly from behind them. 'Maybe you ought to take your own advice and go with it.'

His abruptness surprised Kristin. Seth was invariably polite to his subordinates. She'd even seen him go out of his way to put nervous juniors at ease. But he'd been barely civil with Marco—in fact, it almost seemed as if he was determined to remind the young man of his place.

If that was his plan, it worked well. Marco's face paled a little. 'Sorry, sir,' he said quickly. 'I was only trying to give you and Kristin a feel for the city.'

'What Miss Marshall wants right now,' Seth said, emphasising his more formal use of Kristin's name, 'is to reach her accommodation.'

'Yes, sir. I just thought——'

Seth's voice grew colder. 'I know what you thought, Valenti. What I'm suggesting is that you stop thinking and start driving.'

Marco peered into the rear-view mirror. His easy smile faded.

'Si, Signore.'

The Mercedes whispered through the city, its occupants silent. After a few moments, Kristin pulled down the sun visor and peered into the mirror on its back. She touched her fingers to her hair, as if smoothing it away from her cheeks. But she twisted a little in her seat, until she managed to glimpse Seth's image.

No wonder Marco had retreated, she thought, watching Seth. He was sitting straight as a ramrod, his arms folded across his chest. His face was set in grim lines. Just looking at him was enough to silence anyone.

The pleasant, relaxed man who'd flown with her to Rome had been replaced by the hard-faced stranger she'd glimpsed over the past few weeks. But Marco *had* prattled on; even she'd begun to weary of his chatter.

And Seth was close to exhaustion. Things were catching up to him: the press of last-minute business before they'd left the States, the swiftness of the transfer...

And whatever had happened with Jeanne Lester. That had upset him, too. Hadn't it?

'Kristin?'

She started as Seth leaned forward and put his hand on her shoulder. Their eyes met in the mirror.

'You look exhausted,' he said softly. 'Why don't you close your eyes and rest?'

She smiled. 'I was just thinking the same thing about you.' She looked at the reflections, at his lips close to her ear, at his strong fingers lying possessively against her, and a tremor went through her.

'Yes,' she said, 'that's a good idea.'

Seth sat back and she pushed the mirror aside and lay her head back, deliberately emptying her mind of everything as they drove the rest of the way in silence.

Eventually, Marco pulled the Mercedes to the kerb before a handsome tumble of grey stone.

'Here we are,' he said. 'Your flat is the one on the first level, Kris...' His eyes went to the mirror. 'Signorina Marshall.'

The building was old and lovely. Kristin's curiosity reawakened as she stepped on to the pavement.

'How beautiful,' she said softly. 'Is it Renaissance?'

Marco smiled at her. 'Probably. This whole area dates from that period. I would be very happy to show you——'

Seth's door slammed as he got out of the car.

'Have you the key to your flat, Kristin?'

She turned towards him, her smile fading as she saw his scowling face.

'Yes,' she said. 'It's right——'

He snatched the key from her hand. 'I'll see Miss Marshall to her door. Valenti, get the luggage.'

Seth's hand closed on her elbow, the grip of his fingers hard and certain. Kristin glanced over her shoulder; Marco Valenti was watching them with a strange half-smile on his face.

She felt a fluttery apprehension as he led her inside. The look on Marco's face disturbed her. As for Seth's behaviour, it was more than impolite now. He was acting as if she—as if he...

'Shall I come in?'

Kristin blinked. They were standing in a shadowy, marble-floored hallway. Smiling cherubs looked down on them from rococo wooden mouldings. Ahead, an ornate wood and brass door stood ajar.

She looked up at Seth. His face was still drawn, and in the shadowed light it was impossible to see his eyes. But she sensed something in the way he was watching her, as if he was waiting, waiting...

'No,' she said quickly. 'I'll be fine, thanks.'

'Are you sure?'

His hand was still on her arm. Now, his fingers spread along its surface; she could feel the imprint of each through the jacket of her light wool suit.

'Yes.'

He moved closer to her. She could see his eyes now, and her breath caught. They had gone from hazel to something dark and smoky.

'Kristin.'

His voice was as smoky as his eyes. There was an urgency to the way he'd said her name that sent a rush of pleasure whispering along her skin. His hand slipped up her arm to her shoulder, to the nape of her neck, and she felt the press of his fingers against her naked flesh.

'Seth?'

She whispered his name into the silence. What was she asking him? she thought. To let her go? To take away his hand? No. Not that; she was moving forward under that gentle pressure, her head was tilting back until all she could see was Seth's face.

A shudder went through her as his hand curled around her nape. His head bent to hers; her lashes fell as she felt the warmth of his breath. His hand slid to her throat, his thumb resting against the wild beat of her pulse.

'Kristin,' he said again, urgently this time, and she made a little sound in her throat as he drew her closer. She felt the feathery brush of his lips against her temple, her cheek. His hand curved around her jaw. If she turned her head just a little, she could put her mouth to his skin and taste its heat...

Footsteps clattered loudly on the marble steps and along the hall. Seth's hand fell away from her and Kristin stepped back quickly. Her shoulders hit the wall, and she leaned back against it, grateful for its support, knowing she would surely have fallen if it weren't there.

They stared at each other as Marco, laden with her luggage, rounded the corner.

'Where do you want your luggage, *Signorina*?' he said. She was almost afraid to answer, afraid her voice would tremble. She took a deep breath and somehow drew her eyes from Seth's.

'Right inside the door will be fine, thanks.' She watched as Marco set her luggage in place and then, before either man could say anything, she stepped through the door to her flat. 'I'll see you both tomorrow.' With a quick push, she slammed the door closed and leaned against it until the world stopped spinning away from her.

Finally, she closed the bolt, then turned and wearily surveyed her new home.

Yes, she thought, yes, she really *was* tired. What she needed more than anything was a good, long sleep.

The Harbrace offices were a handsome building off the Via del Corso. Kristin arrived there early the next morning by taxi, before most of the other employees had arrived. But Marco Valenti was already at his desk. He greeted her with a pleasant smile and the offer of a freshly brewed cup of espresso.

'Bless you,' she said, smiling at him over the rim of the cup. 'I've been aching for coffee ever since I woke up.'

He nodded. 'No good Italian would think of starting the day without his coffee.' He sat down on the edge of the desk opposite and looked at her. 'Isn't the boss coming in today?'

'Mr Richards? I'm sure he must be.'

Marco smiled. 'I would have thought you and he would have come in together.'

Kristin looked at him. 'Why would you think that?'

He shrugged. 'His flat is above yours. So I just assumed...'

'Above mine? In the same building, you mean?'

Marco's brows arched. '*Si*. Didn't you know that?'

'No,' she said softly. 'No, I didn't.'

There was a moment's silence, and then he cleared his throat. 'I was thinking—you seemed interested in Renaissance architecture, and I thought perhaps you— perhaps you and I...' He paused. 'I'm not certain how to phrase this,' he said with an uncomfortable little laugh.

Kristin stared at him. 'How to phrase what, Marco?'

'Well, I thought I might show you a little of my city. Your flat is right around the corner from the Piazza Navona, you know. And if it were all right for me to ask you...'

A cool whisper of warning drifted along Kristin's spine. 'What are you trying to say?'

'I don't want to—how do you say? I don't want to step on the toes of *il padrone*, Kristin. So if you—if you and he...' He spread his hands. 'What I am trying to say is that if there is something between you...'

The colour drained from her face. 'I work for Mr Richards,' she said stiffly.

'*Si*. Of course you do—I know that.' Marco shrugged expressively. 'But if there is more than that to the relationship...'

Kristin got to her feet. 'Thank you for the coffee,' she said as she put the cup on his desk.

'Kristin...'

'I'll find my own way,' she said. 'I don't need any help from you.'

'Have I insulted you? *Mi dispiace*—I'm sorry. I had no intention of doing that. It is just that if you and Richards...'

She spun towards him, her face drawn. '*Mr* Richards,' she said sharply. 'is my employer. Do you understand?'

'*Si*. I only meant...'

'I know exactly what you meant. And you're wrong. You're——' She broke off in mid-sentence. Marco was staring at her as if she'd gone crazy. 'I have work to do,' she said as she started towards the door. 'If you'll excuse me...'

'Kristin, *per favore*—I meant no harm. It is just that I saw the way he looked at you. It was—how do you say?—proprietorial, is that the correct word?'

'No,' she said coldly, 'it is not. You're wrong. Very wrong.'

Marco spread his hands. 'It would not be the first time a man and his secretary...'

Kristin paused in the doorway. No, she thought, it wouldn't be. She was living proof of that.

Colour rose in her cheeks. Why was she so angry at Marco? She'd denied the truth to herself, but Seth's behaviour yesterday had, indeed, been proprietorial. She wasn't involved with him, but how was Marco to know that?

In fact, she was lucky he was being this cautious. She had gone down this path before and seen the way employees, especially the men, looked at a woman who was involved with her boss. She'd heard the whispers and snatches of gossip.

'Kristin.' Marco walked to her side and put his hand on her shoulder. 'I apologise again,' he said, turning her gently towards him. 'I don't suppose it would do any good to get down on my knees and beg for forgiveness, would it?' She said nothing, and his hand slipped to her chin. 'I'll even do it in public,' he said, smiling as he tilted her face up, 'in the Piazza Navona, beside the Bernini fountain. And then I'll buy you dinner at the most charming café in all Rome, and we'll walk to the Capitoline. There's a wonderful view across the Forum by moonlight, and——'

'Good morning.'

Seth's voice fell across Marco's like a shadow across the sun. His hand fell away from her as Kristin spun towards the doorway, where Seth stood watching them. His mouth was a slashing line in his dark face.

A sense of unease rose within her.

'Good morning,' she said. She tried to smile, but her mouth had suddenly gone dry, and her lips caught against her teeth. 'Mr Valenti and I were just having coffee.'

'And talking about seeing Rome.' His eyes focused on Marco. 'By moonlight,' he said pleasantly. 'Isn't that right?'

Kristin saw the Adam's apple in Marco's throat rise, then fall.

'Yes, sir,' he said. 'It's something tourists should not miss.'

Seth nodded. 'I'm sure you're right, Valenti.' His teeth glinted in a quick, terrible smile. 'But Miss Marshall isn't a tourist, she's here to work—which is what she'll be doing this evening.'

Kristin stared at him. 'Work? Tonight?'

'Yes. I've a preliminary report to get out.' His eyes met hers. 'Is that a problem?'

'No,' she said slowly. 'No, I suppose it isn't.'

Seth nodded. 'Good,' he said crisply, 'that's settled, then.' He pushed back the sleeve of his pin-striped suit and frowned. 'I'd like to get started, if you please, Kristin. I have some dictation, and then I'd like you to take some notes and fax them to New York.' His eyes swept over Marco in undisguised dismissal. 'Valenti,' he said pleasantly, and then he turned and strode down the hall.

Kristin stood still, trying to come to grips with what had just happened. Seth had treated Marco with barely concealed hostility. He wasn't a fool; he was a sophisticated, educated executive who must know that he was acting badly towards a junior, that he was making his relationship with her seem—seem...

'Kristin?' Seth's voice commanded her presence. She swallowed hard and turned to Marco. He was watching her through narrowed eyes, a knowing little smile on his lips.

Her stomach knotted.

'Marco...'

'Never mind, Kristin. We can always make it another time—say, in the next century, when *il padrone* steps aside.'

A rush of crimson swept into Kristin's face. 'That's uncalled for. I told you, there's absolutely nothing between...'

He sighed. 'Whatever you say—either way, you don't owe me any excuses.'

'I certainly don't. And I'm not offering any. I'm just trying to explain...'

'Try explaining it to yourself, then,' he said gently. 'Because I think you are the only one who doesn't understand.'

'Kristin?'

Seth's demanding voice carried clearly down the hall. Kristin stared at Marco, and then she turned and left the room.

The incident kept playing and replaying in her mind as the day wore on. Seth made no further reference to what had happened; he treated her with the same polite removal as in the past.

But she couldn't stop thinking of how he'd acted towards Marco. Not that his hostility towards the man was any of her concern. Marco Valenti was a big boy, he could fend for himself. As for Seth—if he wanted to antagonise his subordinates, that was his affair.

But her reputation was her affair, and hers alone. She wasn't involved with Seth; it infuriated her to think that on her very first day at a brand-new job such an ugly rumour had already blossomed.

She knew how rumours spread. Marco would say something to someone else, and that someone would mention it to someone else again, and eventually it would cross the Atlantic and arrive in the New York office.

'Kristin?'

She looked up, startled. Seth was standing over her desk, watching her through hooded eyes.

'Is something wrong?'

She looked back at the typewriter. 'No.'

'Are you certain? You've been very quiet, and——'

'I told you, I'm fine.'

Seth perched on the edge of her desk and folded his arms across his chest.

'Maybe you should have taken the day off,' he said, frowning. 'You're probably jet-lagged.'

Kristin's head came up. 'It's nice of you to worry about my welfare,' she said in clipped tones, 'even if it is a little late to bother.'

His brows rose. 'What's that supposed to mean?'

She stared at him for a long moment, and then she shook her head and looked back at the typewriter.

'Nothing,' she said quietly. 'I—I guess maybe I am a little tired.'

She began typing again, her fingers stabbing quickly at the keys although she had no idea of what she was typing. Why was he watching her that way? She could feel the intensity, and suddenly she knew how a deer must feel when it first became aware of the unflinching eye of the wolf.

Seth cleared his throat. 'Why didn't you wait for me this morning? I came to your door at eight—I thought we'd breakfast together.'

'I had no idea our apartments were in the same building,' she said stiffly.

Seth laughed softly. 'Yes. Mrs Dowd seems to have slipped up.'

Kristin lifted her hands from the keyboard and put them in her lap. 'I can't concentrate while you talk,' she said carefully. 'If you want this letter finished today...'

'Forget the letter.' He rose to his feet. 'Why don't you shut down that typewriter while I call a taxi? It's getting late.'

'Late?' Puzzled, she glanced at the clock on the wall behind him. 'It's barely five.'

'I'm still operating on American time,' he said, smiling at her. 'We've put in a long enough day. I thought we'd stop for drinks and then dinner in Trastevere, and then...'

Kristin blinked. 'But you said we had to work late tonight. You told Marco...'

Seth's face darkened. 'Are you complaining, Kristin? Did I spoil your plans for the evening?'

'No. Of course not. But——'

'Get your things,' he said.

'You lied about working late,' she said slowly. 'Didn't you?' He said nothing, and a slow flush rose to her cheeks. 'I don't think I want to go with you, Seth.'

His mouth narrowed. 'And I don't recall giving you a choice.'

'You have no right to give me orders,' she said quietly.

A peal of musical Italian drifted in from the corridor. Seth looked around, then walked to the door and closed it. When he turned back to Kristin, his face was shuttered.

'We have things to talk about,' he said. 'And we can't talk here.'

'Yes. We *do* have things to talk about. What you did this morning—the way you behaved...'

A cold smile curled across his lips. 'Ah,' he said softly. 'I *did* spoil your plans.' He walked towards her and stopped beside the desk. 'Or Valenti's plans, anyway.'

'That was none of your——'

'I told you to get your things, Kristin.'

She hesitated, then nodded.

'All right,' she said. 'But we're going to settle this. You can't treat me as if—as if...'

'As if what?'

The question was softly spoken, but it cried out with the sudden warning of danger.

'As if I were your property,' she said defiantly. 'As if you had some kind of claim on me...'

Seth's eyes grew dark. 'You're wrong,' he said softly. 'I *do* have a claim on you. And we both know it.'

Her heartbeat accelerated. 'I don't know what you're talking about,' she said quickly.

He smiled, and the smile transformed him. The anger was gone, leaving in its place something that set her pulse pounding.

'Kristin.' Her name whispered between them. Seth reached out and clasped her wrist. Heat blazed from that single point of contact, racing along her skin, flaring out through her body until she felt she must be at the centre of a shimmering flame.

She rose to her feet slowly, her eyes locked with his. 'Don't,' she said, but it was too late. She was already in Seth's arms, she was lifting herself on tiptoe and sighing as she pressed herself to him. And when his mouth finally settled hungrily on hers, Kristin knew that this moment had been inevitable.

She and Seth had been moving towards it inexorably—perhaps since the day the world had first begun.

CHAPTER NINE

TIME and place lost all meaning. The feel of Seth's arms as they held her to him, the heat of his mouth—those were the only reality, a reality that made Kristin's dreams pale by comparison.

She would never know how long the kiss lasted. It might have been seconds, it might have been forever—she knew only that the sudden shrill of the telephone washed over her like a spill of icy water.

Her hands fell to Seth's chest and she twisted her face away from his.

'The phone,' she said with a breathless shiver. 'Seth—let me——'

'Let it ring.' His hands slid down her back to her buttocks and he brought her tightly against him. The heat and hardness of his body made her head spin. 'Come back to me and let the damned thing...'

She wrenched free and spun away, then groped blindly on the desk for the phone. Her hand shook as she lifted the receiver.

'Hello?' she said hoarsely, all her office protocol forgotten.

'Kristin?'

It was Marco. Kristin closed her eyes, trying desperately to focus on his voice.

'Marco. Did you—did you want something?'

'Yes. I wanted to apologise again.'

Marco's voice droned on, but she didn't hear him. All her senses were concentrated on Seth. He'd moved quietly behind her, and now his arms were closing around her waist. His hands splayed across her ribs, the tips of his fingers resting just beneath the upward curve of her breasts.

'Hang up the phone,' he said softly, his breath whispering against her temple.

Kristin swallowed hard. 'Marco. I—I'm busy just now. Can I—can I call you back?'

'You sound strange, *cara*. Are you all right?'

Seth bent his head and nuzzled her collar aside. His mouth pressed warmly against her skin, and a tremor went through her.

Her head fell back against his chest and her eyes closed. 'No,' she whispered, 'please...'

'Kristin? I'm having difficulty hearing you,' Marco said. 'Look, I'll come——'

'No.' Her voice was sharp as a gunshot. She twisted free of Seth's embrace and faced him. He was watching her with eyes the colour of molten gold. 'No,' she repeated, 'don't do that, Marco. I—I'm just leaving for the day.'

'What happened to *l'imperatore*? I thought he wanted you to work tonight?'

'He did. But I—I'm jet-lagged. That's why...I'll—I'll see you tomorrow, Marco. All right?'

'*Si*. Perhaps we can have lunch together so I can apologise properly for what happened. I am truly sorry, Kristin—I need your assurance that I am forgiven.'

Kristin closed her eyes. 'You're forgiven,' she said softly. 'Goodbye, Marco.'

'*Ciao,* Kristin. Until tomorrow.'

She hung up the phone and the room filled with silence. Seth took a step towards her.

'Kristin.'

The way he whispered her name made her tremble. But she lifted her chin and met his burning gaze with a cool stare.

'That was Marco,' she said.

Seth made an impatient gesture. 'The hell with——'

'He wanted to apologise,' she said, her voice over-riding his. 'It's just too bad I didn't have the courage to tell him he didn't owe me an apology, that he was right.'

Seth's brows drew together. 'I'm not in the mood for riddles right now. What was he right about?'

A wash of pink rose in her face. 'About you wanting to stake me out as private property.'

Seth's eyes darkened. 'I see. And what happened just now, that was part of it?'

'It wasn't my idea,' Kristin said sharply.

A knowing smile tilted at the corners of his mouth. 'No,' he said softly. 'It was mine. It was about time one of us did something about the way we feel.'

'*We* don't feel...' Her protest died on her lips. It was a lie; she'd melted into his arms; she'd lifted her face eagerly for his kiss, trembled at his caresses.

She sagged back against the desk. 'There's no point in arguing over which of us is the bigger fool,' she said wearily. 'All that matters is that what just happened mustn't happen again.'

Seth smiled. He reached out and put his hand against her cheek. His palm was cool against her fevered skin.

'Is that what you really want, Kristin?'

Their eyes met and held. Finally, however, she managed to nod. 'Yes.'

His hands closed on her shoulders and he drew her to him again. 'I don't believe you,' he said softly, and before she could protest his mouth was on hers. When he finally lifted his head, her heart was racing.

'I want you,' he whispered. His eyes moved slowly over her face. 'Sometimes I think I must have wanted you all my life.'

A flush crept up under Kristin's skin and she looked away from him.

'I'm not going to have an affair with you, Seth,' she said flatly.

His hands slid up her throat and cupped her face. 'Look at me, Kristin.'

'I'll stay until you find someone to replace me. But by next week...'

Her brave words died away as his thumbs traced lightly across the curve of her cheekbones.

'Look at me,' he said again. Slowly, she did as he'd asked. When their eyes met, her heart constricted.

'Seth,' she whispered, 'please—let go of me.'

His eyes searched hers. 'Tell me what you're afraid of.'

'I'm not afraid,' she said quickly. But it was a lie. She *was* afraid; she knew what came next as surely as she knew the steps of a waltz, just as she knew it was as much her fault as his that things had reached this point. It had just been less humiliating to lay the blame solely on him.

She owed him something for that. She owed him honesty.

'Seth.' Kristin forced herself to meet his gaze directly. 'I—I apologise if I misled you. I have no excuses to offer. But the truth is that I don't want to get involved with you. I don't want an affair.'

Seth's mouth curved with wry amusement. 'Amazing,' he said softly. 'You have the answers, even before you've heard the questions.'

'Seth, please. I'm not a child. I know what you want.'

His smile faded. 'Do you?' he asked in a cool voice.

'Yes.' Her chin lifted. 'You want to take me to bed,' she said with deliberate bluntness.

A cold, dangerous look came into his eyes. 'That man you were involved with—what kind of a bastard was he?'

Caught off guard, Kristin could only shake her head. 'What?'

'If that was all he wanted of you, the man was more of a fool than I thought.'

'Seth, please. What has that to do with...'

'Everything.' His grasp tightened. 'You're comparing me to some s.o.b. who didn't deserve you.' He took a step towards her, until they were only a breath apart. 'And you're comparing what's happening between us to your relationship with him.'

'I'm not,' Kristin said as she tried to pull away from him. 'I'm just telling you the truth—I'm doing what I have to do to make you see that...'

Seth's mouth twisted. 'And so will I,' he said tightly as he bent to her and his lips claimed hers.

His mouth was hard, as were his hands as he held her immobilised. She tried twisting away, but he was too strong and determined—and then she felt the fight drain from her. The heat of Seth's kiss flamed through her, igniting not just her body but her soul.

I don't want this, she thought. But Seth sensed the change in her; he muttered something unintelligible and drew her more closely against him, and suddenly her mouth softened beneath his, opening like a flower to the caress of his tongue.

It was Seth who finally ended the kiss, and when he drew back Kristin saw the glitter of triumph in his golden eyes.

'If you only knew how I've dreamed of you.'

A smile trembled on her mouth as she thought of her own dreams. For the moment, her fears were forgotten.

'Have you?' she whispered.

Seth nodded as he traced her softly swollen mouth with the tip of his finger. 'Yes. There've been nights I lay awake until dawn, wondering by what bit of magic you'd come into my life.' A smile curved across his mouth, and he laughed softly. 'I might have got that girl down the hall for my secretary instead of you—you know, the one with a different hair colour each week.'

Kristin's smile trembled. His secretary. *His secretary.*

The word seemed to echo through the room, bringing with it the return of reality.

'Weren't you lucky?' she said, wrenching free of his grasp. 'I don't suppose she'd have tickled your fancy.'

Seth's face darkened. 'Damn it, Kristin...'

'I suppose I should be flattered that you want my body. Don't look at me that way, Seth. It's the truth, isn't it? That's what you want.'

His eyes became pools of golden light. 'Yes,' he said, 'that's right.' His arms closed around her, imprisoning her against him. 'I want to take you to my bed and keep you there until neither of us has the strength to walk.'

'If that's supposed to make me give in to you...'

'I want to kiss your mouth until it's swollen, I want to taste your skin, to make you cry out for release beneath me.'

His whispered words were making her head spin. 'Stop it,' she whispered, 'you have no right to...'

His arms tightened around her, until Kristin could barely catch her breath.

'I want all that,' he said. 'And more.'

Kristin stared at him, her eyes bright with defiance and unshed tears.

'What more could you want?' she demanded.

The seconds ticked away as Seth looked at her, his expression hard and distorted by passion and then, like a mask dropping away, his face softened.

He looked into her eyes and smiled gently.

'The one answer you haven't thought of, Kristin. Love.'

He took her to a little café in Trastevere. It was a very old section of the city, with narrow, twisting cobbled streets and tiny, unexpected piazzas. Opening on one of them was a café so small that the tourists had passed it by.

The night was warm, and Seth chose a table outside, tucked just beneath the overhanging branches of a plane tree. Kristin shook her head when he asked if she was hungry. The thought of trying to force food down her throat made her feel ill. But he ordered something—wine, she thought, as she half listened to the quick exchange of Italian between Seth and the waiter—and then he leaned back in his chair and looked at her.

'I don't know why I let you talk me into this,' she said. 'We don't have anything to say to each other.'

'Don't we?' he said. 'Maybe you didn't hear what I said to you in the office, Kristin.'

She had heard. For one breathless moment, she'd almost let herself believe him. The world had shimmered with happiness. He loves me, she'd thought, and in that explosive instant Kristin admitted that she had somehow, despite the dark experience of her past, fallen head over heels in love with Seth.

But the moment hadn't lasted. Even as he still held her in his arms, she remembered that love was just a word that men used to get what they wanted. Vincent had used it readily—and Seth used it all the time.

'Send two dozen roses to....' The names changed too rapidly to remember. 'Have them enclose a card—you know what to say. The usual will do.'

Yes. She knew. 'Put in a card,' she'd tell the florist, 'and sign it, "Love, Seth".'

The realisation had run through her veins like ice water and she'd tried to step free of Seth's embrace. But he wouldn't let go of her; he wouldn't listen to her protests, and all the while Kristin had been painfully conscious of the footsteps just outside his closed door. Finally, she had agreed to go with him to some quiet place and settle things.

Now, with an open bottle of chilled Frascati between them, she waited for Seth to speak. She was calm now—

the taxi ride, and the walk through the old streets, had given her the chance to gain control of herself.

'What are you thinking?'

Kristin lifted her glass and took a sip of wine. It tasted of sun, earth and rain.

'I was thinking about your florist,' she said steadily, her eyes meeting his.

Seth laughed. 'What?'

'Your florist,' she repeated. 'You know, the one who's probably going to go bankrupt because you've left New York.'

His smile tilted a little. 'If there's some special message in this, Kristin, I'm afraid I'm missing it.'

She took a deep breath, then let it out. 'I think it's pretty clear. You have a lot of women.'

'Kristin——'

'There's no sense in denying it.' She managed a quick, cool smile. 'I'm your secretary, after all. I know all about the Altheas and the Elaines and——'

What remained of his smile faded. 'That makes us even, then.' His voice was cold. 'Although not quite. Hell, all I know about your lover is that he walked out on you.'

Kristin blanched. 'It's not the same thing.'

Seth smiled unpleasantly. 'No. It's not. I didn't live with Althea or whoever the hell it is you're talking about. But you...'

Tell him, she thought, tell him it's not true, tell him...

But to tell him the truth was to court disaster, especially now. There could be no retreat once her last defence had been overrun. Instead, she tossed her head.

'It wasn't the way you make it sound,' she said evenly. 'We—we knew things had ended between us; by the time he left, it was just—it had been over for a long time.'

There was a long silence. 'Are you sure?'

Kristin flushed. 'What is this? I don't have to make excuses to you or apologise for——'

Seth reached across the table and his hand closed over hers. 'No,' he said, 'you don't. That's all in the past—and so is the life I lived before I knew you. That's why I'm not going to apologise or make excuses, either.'

'There wouldn't be much point, would there? I mean, you can't very well lie to me about your women.'

The breath hissed from her as the pressure of his fingers increased.

'Damn it, will you listen? I never pretended to be a candidate for sainthood. But I'm not the tomcat you're making me out to be, either.' He paused. 'I dated a lot of women, yes. But——'

'But they didn't mean a thing to you,' Kristin said with cool sarcasm.

'Yes. No.' Seth cursed sharply. 'You're twisting my words. Of course they meant something to me; I wouldn't have spent time with them if they hadn't. Listen, Kristin, everything isn't always black and white——'

She pulled her hand from his. 'Now you're going to tell me things aren't always what they seem.'

Seth nodded. 'That's right, they're not.'

She gave a bitter little laugh. 'Is this speech something that gets passed along in male genes, do you think, like a taste for football or beer?'

'Listen, I don't know what lies your lover told you. But——'

Her chair squealed as she pushed it back from the table. 'Goodbye, Seth. I'd appreciate it if you'd find someone to take my place as quickly as you can.'

Seth slammed his hand on the table. 'No one can replace you,' he said in a rushed, angry voice. 'Damn it to hell, I'm not going to let you——'

Her eyes filled with tears. 'Goodbye,' she whispered. Quickly, she rose to her feet and fled across the square.

'Kristin! Kristin, come back here!'

The sound of his voice calling after her only made her run more quickly. Ahead, a narrow alley branched off,

weaving deeper into the ancient heart of the quarter. It
was hard to run wearing high heels, and the old cobble-
stones underfoot were gaping and uneven. But on she
ran, ran until the panting sound of her own breath
blocked the sound of Seth's voice behind her. She
stumbled once and almost fell, catching herself only at
the last second—and then, suddenly, her heel caught in
a crack between the stones and she went down in a heap,
her back against a cold stone wall.

Her eyes filled with tears of pain and frustration as
Seth pounded around the corner.

'Kristin! Darling, are you hurt?'

'Get away from me,' she sobbed. 'Damn you, Seth!'

He squatted beside her, and she winced as he lifted
her foot gently to him.

'It's not broken, thank goodness. But you've cut the
skin—you're going to have quite a bruise in a couple of
hours.'

'Just leave me alone, will you, please? Seth—what are
you doing?'

It was a foolish question. What he was doing was
gathering her into his arms, then rising to his feet as if
she were weightless.

'Put your arms around my neck, sweetheart,' he said
softly. She hesitated, but there was nothing else she could
do and finally she looped her arms lightly around him.
'That's the way,' he murmured. He smiled at her. 'You're
beautiful, Kristin. Even with dirt on your cheek and your
stockings torn.'

'They were new stockings,' she whispered. 'And—
and...' She began to weep, tears flooding from her eyes
as if they would never stop. 'I don't give a damn about
the stockings,' she sobbed, 'it's—it's...'

'I know,' Seth said, cradling her to him. His lips
brushed softly over her temple. 'I know, darling. And
it's going to be all right. You'll see.'

'It can't be,' she said, burying her face in his shoulder as he carried her back towards the square. 'How can it be all right when I can't want—I don't want...?'

I don't want you, she tried to say. But the words wouldn't come. How could she lie while she was in Seth's arms, cradled against his heart?

A taxi cruised slowly towards the square. Seth hailed it, then settled her carefully into the back seat and got in beside her.

'Look at me,' he said, drawing her into the curve of his arm.

Kristin shook her head. 'No,' she whispered. But he was persistent. Slowly, gently, he lifted her face to his until she was looking at him. In the shadowy light, his eyes were impossible to read. But he was smiling tenderly; she could see the upward curve of his mouth.

'Do you really want me to let you go back to New York?'

The question caught her by surprise. 'I—I... Yes. Of course.'

He nodded solemnly. 'All right, then. I will.' Seth bent his head and kissed her slowly and deeply. 'All you have to do,' he said when he took his mouth from hers, 'is tell me that you don't feel anything for me.'

Kristin's heart skipped a beat. 'That's crazy.'

He shook his head. 'No, it's not. It's very simple. Just look me in the eye, say you don't love me, and I'll take you straight back to your flat and make the arrangements myself.'

'Seth. Don't be silly. Why should I...?'

'I'm waiting, Kristin.'

'Please. This doesn't...'

Seth curled his fingers around her jaw and lifted her face to his. 'Look at me,' he said. Slowly, Kristin did as he'd asked. 'Now,' he said, watching her, 'tell me.'

'Seth...'

'Say it, Kristin.'

I don't love you, she thought. The words were simple enough.

'I—I...' She swallowed. 'I...'

'Well? All you have to say is "Seth, I don't love you," and you're on your way back to the States.'

Kristin swallowed hard. 'All right.' She drew in a deep breath. 'Seth,' she said, looking into his eyes, 'I don't— I don't...'

She fell silent. She had lied to him about having a lover; she had lied to him about not wanting to have him make love to her—but she could never lie about this. Not—not when he was so close. Not when his mouth was a kiss away from hers...

Seth whispered her name and began kissing her, light little kisses that seemed to be drawing the very heart from within her breast.

'Tell me,' he said against her mouth.

Kristin closed her eyes. 'Seth...'

'Tell me,' he insisted, while his hands skimmed lightly over her compliant body in the darkness.

A tremor went through her. She knew what he wanted to hear. It was what she wanted to say, what she'd longed to say for weeks. For months. For all her life.

'Kristin. Say it.'

'I love you,' she sighed. His arms tightened around her. 'I love you,' she said again, 'oh, Seth, I...'

His mouth dropped to hers with a hunger that matched her own. It was going to be all right, she thought. Seth wasn't Vincent, any more than she was Althea or Elaine or any of the others.

A fierce joy rose within her. He could have had any of them, but he'd chosen her.

Not Jeanne, a little voice suddenly whispered inside her head. Not Jeanne, Kristin. He couldn't have her.

Kristin stiffened. She tried to hold back so she could think, but it was too late. Her dreams were finally coming true, and Seth was kissing her over and over again. The little voice became smaller and smaller and further and further away, until finally it faded into the silence of the Roman night.

CHAPTER TEN

KRISTIN threw open the bedroom window and looked out on the bright autumn morning. It was Saturday, and the street was deserted. An elderly woman walking a small dog came around the corner, looked up, and smiled.

'*Buon giorno,* Signorina Marshall. *Come stai?*'

Kristin waved and smiled back. '*Va bene, Signora Giuliano. Grazie.*'

The *Signora*, who lived just down the hall, beamed happily. 'You see?' she said. 'What did I tell you? One week you are here, and already you are sounding like a Roman.'

Kristin laughed. It was an extravagant compliment, one she knew she didn't deserve, but it pleased her anyway.

'*Grazie,*' she said.

'It is going to be a lovely day.' The *Signora* reached down and patted her little dog. '*Bambino* and I are going to the Borghese Gardens. Have you seen them?'

'Not yet, I'm afraid.'

'But you must. You are most welcome to join us, if you like.'

Kristin smiled. 'Thank you. Another time, perhaps.'

The *Signora* nodded wisely. 'Ah,' she said, 'I didn't realise. Your young man is back, yes? The gentleman on the next floor?'

A flush rose to Kristin's cheeks. 'Oh, but he's not my——'

'He will surely take you somewhere romantic on such a day as this, eh?'

132

'No. I mean, he's not back. Besides, he isn't——'

'*Bambino*, you bad dog.' The *Signora* sighed dramatically. 'Forgive me, my dear, but *Bambino* says I must walk him quickly or else he will not be responsible for his actions. *Ciao*.'

Kristin nodded absently, then turned away from the window. Her Roman neighbours knew more about her in a week than the ones back home had ever learned. Things were different here: people went out of their way to be friendly. In New York, you might live in the same apartment building for years and never exchange more than a nod with your neighbours.

The Italian way was charming, Kristin thought as she padded barefoot across the bedroom, but there was something to be said for urban anonymity. At home no one would have noticed that Seth and she knew each other, much less cared about their relationship.

She picked up the hairbrush and began brushing her hair. Her hand stilled as she gazed at her reflection. Who could blame the *Signora* for thinking what she did? The old woman had been walking her dog the night she and Seth had returned from Trastevere. She'd seen him help Kristin from the taxi, then hold her close in the curve of his arm as they made their way from the street to the building entrance.

Kristin's eyes darkened with memory. For all she knew, the *Signora* had even seen the way Seth had swept her up into his arms at the steps, the way he'd kissed her as he climbed them.

What she couldn't know was that the evening had ended at the door to Kristin's flat.

Seth had lowered her gently to her feet, then smiled down at her. 'May I come in?' he'd asked softly.

Kristin's heart turned over. Until that moment, she hadn't let herself think about where the heated kisses and caresses they'd shared in the taxi would lead. Now, faced with what would surely happen next, she suddenly knew that she wasn't ready to take that step.

'This is too new,' she murmured, avoiding his eyes. 'I—I need time to think. Would you mind...?'

He hesitated, and then he whispered her name and tilted her face up to his.

'Yes,' he said, tempering his words with a quick smile, 'I do mind. Very much.' He gave her a long, gentle kiss. 'But I understand, darling.'

Her sense of relief was almost overwhelming. 'Thank you, Seth.'

He traced the contour of her mouth with his thumb. 'How does your ankle feel?'

'Better. Much better.'

He smiled. 'What Dr Richards prescribes is a long hot bath, some aspirin, and a good night's sleep.' He dropped a light kiss on her forehead. 'We'll have breakfast together in the morning.'

The prescription was a good one. But Kristin didn't manage the night's sleep. She kept thinking about the morning, almost dreading Seth's knock at the door.

What would she do if he took her in his arms? There was no sense in trying to pretend she didn't want him to make love to her. She did. She loved him with an intensity that made what she'd felt for Vincent pale by comparison.

But as the night faded to morning, Kristin's doubts became more and more insistent.

Was she really ready to become Seth's lover? Because that was what it came down to, when all was said and done. He hadn't talked of marriage, of any kind of legitimacy.

Neither had Vincent, a little voice agreed.

Kristin shifted uneasily in the tangled sheets. That wasn't fair. Seth wasn't Vincent.

Let him prove it, the voice said.

But that wouldn't be fair. Her doubts were her own, not his.

Still, only a fool would ignore the similarities.

And what about Jeanne Lester? the voice asked.

What about her? Was Jeanne Lester more important than the other women Seth dated?

The little voice chuckled softly. He wanted her to come to Rome with him. That makes her more important, doesn't it?

Was that true? Did it?

Ask him, the voice said. Just ask him.

By morning, she felt exhausted. And then Fate, in the guise of a night cable from one of Harbrace's most important clients, offered a reprieve. She found a note under her door, from Seth. It said that he'd been called away by urgent business in Milan.

'I'll see you next week,' he'd written. 'This is going to be the longest week of my life.'

At first, Kristin welcomed the chance to have some time alone and think things through. But, as the days passed, she went from being grateful for Seth's absence to missing him with a desperation that left her feeling uneasy.

She wasn't ready to feel this way about him. She had lost control of her own life once; the thought of having it happen again was terrifying. Loving someone was like standing, blindfolded, at the edge of a precipice, your hand in his. Would he lead you safely to the other side? Or would he flinch at the responsibility, step back at the last minute, and watch as you tumbled into the abyss?

She knew Seth missed her, too. Not a day passed without some special message.

He sent a portfolio of memos to the office one morning. Tucked in among them, Kristin found a silk scarf in shades of darkest violet.

'For Kristin,' the card with it said, 'whose eyes are a colour that puts this silk to shame.'

A box of tiny, hand-dipped chocolate hearts was waiting for her at her flat one evening. The note with it said, 'For Kristin, who already owns my heart.'

The next night, there was a bottle of Dom Perignon at her door.

'We'll drink this when I come back to you,' the note that accompanied it said.

The notes, more than the gifts, made her heart soar. They weren't the impersonal little jottings she'd so often dictated to Seth's florist on his behalf, no meaningless 'To Kristin—Love, Seth.'

But neither the gifts nor the notes brought her any closer to a decision.

The days dragged on. Marco took advantage of Seth's absence to drop into her office several times each day. He was pleasant and never referred to Seth while urging Kristin to let him take her to dinner.

'No strings, as you Americans say,' he insisted pleasantly, 'just a good meal and agreeable conversation.'

But his eyes told another story, and Kristin turned him down. There might still be uncertainty in her mind about what road to take with Seth, but she knew that what she felt for him was more real than the earth beneath her feet.

She would give her heart to Seth, or to no one.

The week had finally ended. Now it was Saturday, and she was no closer to an answer than she'd been on Monday. Sighing, Kristin smoothed the bed cover into place. At least she had the weekend left. Maybe she could sort things out before...

The chime of the doorbell made her start. Signora Giuliano, Kristin thought as she padded to the front door. She probably wanted to urge her to change her mind about going to the Gardens. Well, maybe she would. It really was a lovely day; it wouldn't hurt to get out for a couple of hours.

Smiling, Kristin pulled the door open. 'All right,' she said, tossing back the dark hair that streamed over her shoulders, 'I've changed my mind. I'd love to go to...'

But it was not the *Signora* who stood in the doorway, it was Seth, in suit and tie, his flight bag and briefcase beside him.

Her heart soared. 'Seth. I thought you were in Milan.'

'Did you?' His tone was clipped, his eyes cool as they swept over her sleep-tangled hair and her bathrobe. 'Were you expecting someone, Kristin? Or has he just departed?'

Her welcoming smile dimmed. 'I thought you were my neighbour,' she said slowly.

'How charming. Your neighbour joins you for breakfast, hmm? And invites you out for the day as well. Is that what you'd like me to believe?'

Kristin's chin tilted up. 'Yes,' she said, staring at him. 'Although, on second thought, I don't much care whether you believe it or not. Goodbye, Seth.'

A look of anguish spread across his face. 'Kristin.' He caught the door as she started to push it shut. In one easy motion, he stepped past it and pulled her into his arms. 'Forgive me,' he whispered. 'I'm a jealous fool. But I've missed you so badly. So...'

Seth's mouth dropped to hers, his kiss filled with the hunger of the days that had separated them. Kristin held back for a moment and then her arms went around his neck.

'You've nothing to be jealous of,' she whispered. 'Don't you know that?'

She felt the tension drain from his body. 'I told you,' he said, 'I'm a fool.' He smiled and leaned his forehead against hers. 'Did you miss me?'

'Yes,' she admitted, 'every minute.'

His arms tightened around her. 'I couldn't bear the thought of being without you for the weekend, so I rushed things in Milan. I said I had urgent business in

Rome.' He kissed her. 'And I do,' he whispered. His
hands slid to the open collar of her robe. 'I do, Kristin.'

A sweet ache spread through her belly and breasts.
She swayed as his fingers stroked her throat. She wanted
to touch him, too, to put her hands beneath his shirt
and feel the heat of his flesh.

But she couldn't. Not yet.

Her hands clasped his wrists. 'Seth,' she said. 'Don't.'

He laughed softly. 'I won't. Not here, in the hallway,
at any rate.' He stepped inside the flat and closed the
door behind him. 'Let me look at you,' he said, clasping
her elbows and holding her at arm's length. His gaze
moved over her slowly, the warmth of it heating her body.
'God,' he said in a thick voice, 'you're so beautiful,
Kristin.'

She swallowed past the lump that had suddenly lodged
in her throat. She couldn't think straight, not when he
looked at her that way.

'Seth . . .'

But he wasn't listening. He was looking at her as if
he'd never seen her before.

'I love your hair loose that way,' he murmured. Her
breath caught at his touch. 'It feels like silk against my
fingers.'

His hands were at her waist, untying the sash to her
robe. It fell open, revealing the pale pink nightgown she
wore beneath. The fine silk clung lightly to her body,
and a tremor went through her as she saw the sudden
darkening of Seth's eyes.

'This is how I dreamed you'd look,' he said. 'So proper
in the office—and like this when you were dressed just
for me.' She gasped as he reached out and cupped her
breast over the silk gown. 'Do you want me, Kristin?'
Passion hardened the angles of his face. 'You do,' he
said softly. 'I can see it.'

She bit her lip and looked down at herself as his hand
drifted across her. There was no way to hide her desire:

it was visible in the hard thrust of her swollen breasts beneath their silk covering, in the way her body swayed towards him.

'Seth.' Her voice was a thready whisper. Somehow, she found the strength to grasp the lapels of her robe and draw them together. 'Seth,' she said again, 'let's— let's go somewhere.'

He raised his head and looked at her like a man emerging from a deep sleep.

'What?'

'I said...' She swallowed. 'I said, it's such a beautiful day that I thought—I thought we'd...' Her eyes met his. 'Let's—let's just spend some time getting to know each other.'

She could hear the rasp of his breath in the silence. When he finally spoke, his voice was rough.

'All right.' Her eyes closed as he ran his hand along her cheek, and then he stepped away from her. 'I'm going to my flat and change my clothes. I'll be back for you in fifteen minutes.' He bent to her and kissed her hard. 'Fifteen minutes, darling,' he whispered. 'But if you're still dressed as you are right now, the only place we're going is to bed.'

She had dreamed of this place, Kristin thought as she walked slowly alongside Seth through the grounds of the Villa d'Este. The sixteenth-century villa sprawled along the hills outside Rome, with formal gardens sweeping down a slope in an endless fall of terraces to reflecting pools below. There were fountains everywhere, hundreds of them, and the play of water over stone was like a living sculpture.

'Glad we came?' Seth asked softly.

Kristin looked up at him and smiled. 'Yes. It's wonderful.'

He took her hand and laced their fingers together. 'Now—tell me what's worrying you.'

'Nothing is . . .' She sighed. 'Am I that transparent?'

He smiled. 'I'm only just beginning to realise I've stored up all kinds of information about you over the past months.' His hand squeezed hers. 'Your eyes turn a smoky shade of violet when you're worried about something.' He leaned down and kissed her temple. 'Just the way they are now.'

Kristin drew a deep breath. 'It's just—things happened so quickly, Seth. I—I think we ought to slow down a little.'

His arm slipped around her waist. They walked in silence for a few minutes, and then he sighed.

'I don't mean to rush you into anything,' he said softly. 'It's just that we've wasted so many damned months being "Mr Richards" and "Miss Marshall".'

Kristin smiled up at him. 'When did you first see me?' she asked. 'Really see me, I mean.'

Seth smiled. 'I don't know, exactly. The night we went for pizza. Or maybe it was the afternoon I found you wrestling with the typewriter ribbon.' He drew her closer to him. 'When did you first look past the "Mr Richards" and see me?'

She shrugged her shoulders. 'I'm not certain. I thought it was that night we had pizza, too.' A smile tilted slowly across her mouth. 'But when I think back, I realise that I must have been storing up little bits of information about you, too.'

'Like what?'

Her smile broadened. 'Like the fact that you're grumpy as a bear before you have your morning coffee.'

'Me?' he said in wounded tones.

Kristin laughed. 'You, Mr Richards.'

Seth grinned. 'OK, maybe it's true.' They made their way past a rushing fountain and down to the next terrace. 'Go on. What else?'

'I know that blue's your favourite colour.'

'Don't tell me that's in my personnel file!'

Kristin leaned her head against his shoulder. 'You seem to own ten blue ties for every red or grey one.' She looked up at him. 'Now what do you suppose that means?' she asked with great innocence.

He laughed. 'It means, Miss Marshall, that you're a very perceptive secretary. Well, keep going. How many of my other secrets have you discovered?'

Kristin's smile wavered a little. 'Not nearly enough.'

'My life's an open book,' Seth said lightly. 'What do you want to know?'

'Everything,' she said. Ask him about Jeanne Lester, she thought. Ask him if Jeanne had really mattered to him.

'Everything,' he repeated. 'Hmm.' He took her hand in his and swung it as they strolled. 'OK, everything it is. Let's see. I come from a little town you've probably never heard of called Emerson, Colorado.'

Kristin laughed. 'You're absolutely right. I never have.'

'Population three thousand on a good day. I grew up in a house tucked against the Rockies, with the requisite mother and two fathers, one baby sister, three dogs...'

She came to an abrupt halt. '*How* many fathers?' she demanded.

Seth grinned. 'I thought that might get your attention. Two. The one who gave me life, and the one who raised me—my stepfather. My real father died when I was eight.'

'That must have been rough.'

'It was. But my stepfather is a great guy. He came along a couple of years later, and pretty soon he and my mother presented me with a sister.'

'How kind of them,' Kristin said with a smile.

Seth nodded. 'Yeah, I thought so, too. She was better than any puppy I'd ever had. She followed me around and she thought everything I said or did was wonderful. Until...' His voice died away.

'Until?' Kristin prompted.

'Until she grew up, and decided she knew it all.'

'Sounds like a typical American girl to me,' she said teasingly.

'Yes.' His voice seemed suddenly cool. 'I thought you might say that.'

She glanced up at him. 'What's that supposed to mean?'

Seth looked at her in silence, and then he shrugged. 'It just means that you women all stick together,' he said lightly. 'You always do.'

'And you'd know all about women, wouldn't you?'

Kristin had meant the words to sound as teasing as his. But somehow they hadn't come out that way. Seth stopped walking and turned her towards him.

'Do I?' he said, his eyes on hers. 'Then why are you asking?'

She swallowed drily. 'I just—I just can't help but wonder why you want me, Seth,' she said. 'I'm not like the women you know.'

A smile curved across his mouth. 'No,' he said softly, 'no, you aren't.'

'What we said before, about not knowing very much about each other—it's true, you know. I mean, we—we don't know about each other's past involvements or...or...'

Seth's eyes narrowed. 'Listen to me,' he said, his hands cupping her shoulders. 'I don't believe in playing true confessions. I told you the other night, I wasn't a saint.' His mouth twisted. 'And I don't expect you to have been one, either.' He gazed into her eyes, and then he kissed her tenderly. 'But I don't want to talk about the past. There's nothing we have to tell each other that matters, darling. Do you understand?'

Kristin stared at him. His message was clear enough. He didn't want to answer questions about the women he'd known, and he was granting her the same right of silence.

A weight lifted from her heart. Goodbye, Jeanne, she thought. And goodbye, at long last, to Vincent.

A smile tilted across her mouth. 'I understand.' She put her hands on his chest, lifted her face to his, and kissed him.

Seth's breath caught. 'That's the first time you've kissed me,' he said.

'I love you,' she said softly.

He looked deep into her eyes, and then he put his arm around her shoulders.

'Let's go home,' he said.

Kristin didn't hesitate. 'Yes,' she said, 'let's.'

Hours later, as the setting sun dusted the cobblestoned streets with gold, Kristin glanced across her living-room and smiled. Seth lay sprawled on the sofa, sound asleep.

By the time they'd reached her flat he'd been yawning.

'Forgive me, darling,' he'd apologised. 'I didn't get much sleep the last few days.'

Kristin had insisted he sit down while she made coffee, and he'd finally given in.

'I'm just going to loosen my tie,' he'd called after her as she headed into the kitchen.

When she'd returned to the living-room, she'd found him asleep, sitting straight up on the sofa, his jacket off and tie open. She'd watched him, then put down the coffee-cups and walked to his side.

'Seth?' she'd whispered.

But the even rise and fall of his chest had been undisturbed. After a moment, Kristin had smiled and knelt beside him. Carefully, she'd slipped his shoes from his feet, then eased him down on the sofa. He'd gone willingly, rolling on to his side, murmuring something unintelligible when she draped a light blanket over him.

Then she'd settled in a chair opposite with a book.

But she didn't do much reading. What did a book mean, a make-believe world filled with make-believe people, when reality was sleeping on a sofa across the room?

Seth, she thought, turning his name over in her mind, tasting it on her tongue as if it were some rare and glorious spice. It was wonderful to have him here—she'd missed him more than she'd imagined. And he'd missed her, too: he was worn out from rushing things in Milan so that he could get back to her.

Kristin let the book fall closed. She could spend the next thousand Saturdays like this, she thought dreamily, going to the park or the museum, then coming home and sitting quietly with Seth...

His sudden cry rent the silence. Kristin jumped up and hurried to him. He'd come bolt upright on the sofa. His eyes were open, but they were wide and unseeing.

'Seth,' she said softly. 'Darling, wake up.'

The muscles in his neck stood out as he twisted his head from side to side. 'Come with me,' he mumbled. 'I can't leave you...'

Her heart turned over. What was he dreaming? And who was he dreaming of? Just as her brain began searching for the answer, his eyes opened.

'Kristin?'

'You were having a nightmare,' she said, staring at him.

He stared at her. 'Yes,' he said finally, 'I...' He sat up and ran his hands over his face. 'I feel like hell.'

'I guess—I guess the dream really upset you,' she said slowly.

Seth looked at her. 'Yes,' he said after a minute. A muscle knotted in his jaw. 'Yeah, I guess it did.' He got to his feet. 'I'm sorry, Kristin. I didn't mean to sleep the day away.'

Kristin shook her head. 'No, that's all right,' she said. She gave him a quick smile. 'Really, I didn't mind.'

Seth took her hand and brought her to him. 'Hey,' he said softly, 'why such a long face?' She didn't answer, and he smiled and kissed the tip of her nose. 'I know what's wrong with you,' he said. 'You're probably starved. Look, why don't I go up to my flat and shower and change? I'll pick you up in an hour or so, and——'

'But you're tired.'

Seth smiled. 'Let me worry about that. You just put on your very best dress. We're going out to see Rome.' He drew her into the warm circle of his arms. 'Unless you'd like to take that shower with me?'

She laughed softly. 'Go on. I'll be ready in an hour.'

Seth grinned. 'You'd better be.'

Showered, her hair blown dry and gleaming like silk as it hung down her back, Kristin stood before the wardrobe in her bedroom, staring at the row of neat suits that hung there. With a little smile, she reached past them to the black dress Susan had convinced her to take along.

She slipped it over her head and stepped into the strappy high-heeled silver shoes that complemented the sequins scattered across the bodice. Her eyes widened when she looked into the mirror.

Who was this woman with the creamy, bare shoulders and the bright colour in her cheeks? She looked—she looked beautiful.

It was what Seth said when she opened the door a few minutes later.

'Beautiful,' he whispered.

It was how he looked, too, Kristin thought as she looked shyly at this handsome stranger in a black dinner suit.

He took her in his arms, kissed her, then put her from him and smiled.

'This is our first date,' he said. 'Do you realise that, Miss Marshall?'

Kristin smiled. 'We've already had our first date,' she said. 'You took me for pizza, remember?'

Seth grinned as he tucked her hand into the crook of his arm. 'I think you'll like the place we're going this time even better.'

She liked it all: the charming restaurant set on an ancient piazza, the candle-lit tables, the walk afterwards through the cobblestoned streets of the old city.

Marco had promised her the Capitoline Hill by moonlight; but it was Seth who took her there, Seth who drew her into his arms as the moon cast its ancient eye over the ghosts of the Caesars in the Forum below.

And later, under that same benevolent gaze, Seth and Kristin stepped softly into her flat.

'Thank you for a lovely evening,' Kristin whispered.

'You're welcome,' Seth said softly as he cupped her face and lifted it to him.

Their kiss was long and dizzying, and it ended only to begin again.

'I want to make love to you, Kristin,' he whispered against her mouth.

Kristin looked up at him in the moonlit room. He was waiting for her to give him some sign of what she wanted.

And this time, she knew.

She took his hand and brought it to her breast. Seth made a sound deep in his throat that was part triumph, part desire.

'My love,' he said. 'Kristin, my love.'

She caught her breath as he reached behind her and pulled down her zipper. The black dress fell away from her, leaving her in a black lace teddy.

Seth put his hand to her cheek, her throat, to the rising curve of her breasts.

'Undress me,' he whispered.

Kristin's hands trembled as she slid his jacket from his shoulders, then undid his tie. She hesitated, and Seth caught her hand in his and brought it to his mouth, turning it so that his lips pressed against her palm. His kiss was hot against her skin.

'I love you,' she sighed. Her hands lifted; she clasped his face. His shadowy beard was abrasive against her skin. Kristin lifted herself to him, her mouth opening beneath his as he kissed her, and then she drew back and slowly unbuttoned his white shirt.

When the shirt fell away, Kristin stroked her palms over the fine mat of dark hair that curled across his flesh, touched the silken skin that stretched tautly across his muscled shoulders and arms.

Seth moaned her name and caught her face between his hands. 'This is the way it was always meant to be for us.' She closed her eyes as his mouth took hers. 'Always, from the very beginning.'

He was right. Oh, yes, he was right. Pleasure was curling like smoke through her blood, spreading in dizzying waves with each heavy beat of her heart.

His hands stroked lightly over the lace teddy. This is a dream, she thought, closing her eyes, a dream like all the others.

But the touch of his hands on her breasts, the silken feel of his skin, the heat of his mouth—all of it was real. Seth was real. He was the man she had waited for all her life.

He put his hands on her hips and drew her towards him, whispering her name in a husky voice so drugged with need and desire that it sent a shudder through her. She moaned as he leaned forward and kissed her breast through the lace that covered it, then touched his tongue lightly to the hardened nipple beneath.

Kristin began to tremble. Seth lifted his head and looked at her. His fingers tangled in the hair at the nape of her neck and he bent her head back, kissing her mouth until it felt swollen and bruised. His lips moved to her throat, to the swell of her breast, then down the lace teddy that had already been moistened by his mouth.

He dropped to his knees before her. 'You're so beautiful,' he whispered.

Seth cupped her buttocks and brought her to him. She cried out as he buried his face against her belly. She felt the heat of his breath, and then the touch of his mouth flamed through the thin fabric that still covered her.

'Seth.' Her voice broke. 'Seth, my love.'

He rose and swept her into his arms. The darkness swirled around her as he carried her to the bedroom.

Moonlight rippled across the bed like a silver river. Seth lay her down, then gently stripped away the teddy, his hands moving slowly across her body.

'Kristin,' he said thickly. She opened her eyes slowly. 'Watch me,' he whispered, 'watch me make love to you, darling.'

His dark head bent to her again, and she drew a dizzying breath as his mouth moved slowly along her flesh. His kisses were flame against her throat, her breasts, the rounded convexity of her belly. She whimpered softly when he parted her legs and stroked the tender skin of her inner thighs, and then his mouth was against her, seeking out her secret flesh.

Pleasure so intense it was almost pain shot through her. Her eyes closed, her head fell back; radiant colours danced against her eyelids, bedazzling her senses.

'Tell me you want me,' he whispered.

Kristin's eyes opened slowly. She looked at Seth as he knelt over her, and her arms opened wide.

Smiling, his gaze never leaving hers, he rose to his feet and unzipped his trousers, pushed them down, and stepped free of them.

He was powerful in his maleness, a marble god made flesh. She reached out as he came to her: she wanted to touch him, to learn all the secrets of his transfiguration.

But she was on fire for him. At the first brush of his skin against hers, she knew that all the rest could wait until she'd known Seth's possession.

She moaned as he moved over her and caught her to him. And when finally he entered her, she cried out.

'What is it, love?' he whispered.

There was so much she wanted to say. She longed to tell him that she had been hurting for years, that in this one moment he had healed her, he had erased all the anguish and pain and given her back herself.

But words were impossible. The past was dead, Seth had said, and he was right. She was beyond speech, anyway; she was following him up a long, spiralling staircase that led into the night sky and to the crystalline radiance of the moon.

In the end, she could only show him, show him and make him know that she wanted what was happening to go on and on forever.

And it did, throughout the long, silken heat of the Roman night, ending only to begin again. When dawn painted the city a fiery pink, Kristin finally curled into Seth's arms and tumbled into a dark dreamless sleep.

CHAPTER ELEVEN

SUNLIGHT, reaching through the latticed shutters, painted Kristin's skin with stripes of gold. She sighed in her sleep and rolled on to her stomach.

'Mmm,' she murmured drowsily.

'Mmm, indeed,' a deep voice whispered. A hand brushed gently across her naked shoulders, down her spine, then cupped her bottom.

'I'm asleep,' she protested as she snuggled deeper into the pillows.

Seth laughed softly. 'But not for long,' he said, turning her into his arms. He smiled down at her as she blinked her eyes open. 'Good morning, love.'

Kristin smiled back at him. 'Good morning,' she said softly.

They kissed, and then Seth drew back. 'I thought I'd never get you up,' he said with a mock frown. 'Here it is, eight o'clock...'

She groaned and threw her arm over her eyes. 'Eight o'clock? Why are we awake at such an ungodly hour on a Sunday morning?'

'Because it's the Christians versus the Lions at the Colosseum,' he said, dropping kisses on her upturned wrist, 'and Caesar's giving a reception at the Pantheon.' He grinned as she groaned again. 'First, I thought we might have breakfast.'

Kristin's eyes flew open. 'Did somebody mention breakfast?' she said innocently.

Seth laughed. 'I thought that might do it, you lazy wench.' He rose to his feet, and Kristin's eyes opened wider when she realised he was wearing softly faded jeans and a pale grey sweater.

'You're dressed,' she said.

'Ah, *Signorina*, how observant you are.' He held up one finger. *'Un momento, per favore.'* She smiled as he backed dramatically from the room. Less than a minute later, he returned, holding his hands behind him. 'Which hand first? Right or left?'

'Umm—the right one.'

With a grand flourish, he held out an old-fashioned nosegay of violets. Kristin struggled up against the pillows.

'Where on earth...?'

Seth grinned. 'It wasn't easy, believe me. Rome sleeps in on Sundays.'

She took the flowers and buried her face in them. Violets, she thought happily. Not roses or orchids— violets.

'They're beautiful.'

He smiled. *'Va bene.* And now, *Signorina*, for the left hand.' Another flourish, and a steaming cup of espresso appeared.

'Lovely,' Kristin said, reaching towards him. 'I thought I smelled coffee, but I was afraid it was just wishful thinking.'

Seth held the cup just out of reach. 'Another good-morning kiss,' he said. 'Then you can have your espresso.'

She smiled and lifted her face to his. After a long moment, he handed the cup to her and watched as she took her first sip.

'Delicious,' she said.

'Not as delicious as you.'

She smiled again. 'If you keep flattering me, I may just get up and make us some breakfast—although there's not very much in the house. I was going to shop yesterday, but...'

Seth whisked a Kleenex from the box beside the bed and draped it dramatically over his arm.

'And what, pray tell, would the *Signorina* like for breakfast, eh?' he said with his very best Italian accent. 'Some cheese? Fruit? Some fresh-baked bread?'

'Yes, yes and yes. But I'm afraid the cupboard is bare.'

Seth grinned. 'It's not bare any more. We have *provolone*, fresh *mozzarella*, figs, peaches...'

'You went shopping at this hour?' Kristin smiled. 'How nice. Thank you.'

He shook his head as he took the cup and the flowers from her and put them aside.

'You'll have to do better than that,' he said softly, and suddenly she was in his arms.

'How's that?' she whispered breathlessly when the kiss ended.

'It's a start,' he said, burying his face against her throat. 'But I think a man who gets out of a warm bed to scour the streets for bread and flowers for his lady love deserves more.'

Kristin leaned back against the pillows. 'You didn't have to get up and get dressed just for me.' A flush rose along her skin. 'I mean...'

Seth's eyes glinted wickedly. 'Watch how easily that's remedied,' he said as he got to his feet.

His shirt flew across the room, and then his shoes. She was laughing by the time he unbuckled his belt. 'Seth, for heaven's sake—what are you doing?'

Naked, he fell down on the bed beside her.

'Breaking the world's record for undressing,' he said, laughing along with her. 'Well, what do you think? Did I make it into the record books?'

'How should I know, you crazy man?'

Kristin's breath caught as their eyes met. Seth's smile tilted and he reached out and slowly drew the blanket from her breasts. 'I thought we'd try for a different record this time,' he said thickly, 'one based on seeing how long we can do this.' He bent over her and kissed her mouth. 'And this.' His head dropped to her breast and he drew her nipple into his mouth. 'And this,' he whispered, his eyes holding hers as his hand moved under the blanket. Desire hardened his face. 'How does that sound?'

'It sounds—it sounds...' Kristin moaned as he touched her, and then she wound her arms around Seth's neck and drew him down to her. And then, for a long time, there were no words at all.

They spent the day in, sometimes making love, sometimes talking, but never more than a hand-span apart. They feasted on the foods Seth had bought and washed it all down with a bottle of Soave he brought down from his flat.

In the evening, they showered together, dressed, and went out, holding hands as they walked the quiet streets until they stumbled on a little trattoria where Seth ordered *pasta al vongole* and a bottle of Chianti Classico.

Their meal arrived, the pasta heaped into huge bowls, overflowing with tiny Mediterranean clams in their shells.

'I'll never eat all that,' Kristin said. But she did, and when she finished, she sighed. 'It must have been all that walking before dinner that gave me such an appet——'

She broke off, blushing, as Seth began to chuckle. 'It would be nice if you gave credit where credit is due,' he said.

'You're terrible,' she said, but she was smiling.

He leaned across the table and kissed her lightly, and then he pushed back his chair and got to his feet.

'Come on, woman. I'm going to buy you the best *gelati* in town.'

They walked to a little shop near the Spanish Steps where they ate the creamiest ice-cream Kristin had ever tasted, and then they finished the evening sitting at a pavement café on the Via Veneto, where they sipped tiny cups of dark rich espresso.

When they finally returned to Kristin's flat, it was very late. Seth held out his hand for her key, unlocked the door, then took her in his arms. He leaned his forehead against hers and smiled.

'This,' he said softly, 'has been the most wonderful day of my life.'

'Mine, too,' Kristin answered. 'Thank you, Seth.'

He brushed his lips lightly over hers. 'No, *Signorina*, it's I who must thank you. I've been in Rome before—many times.' He traced the outline of her mouth with his index finger. 'But the city has never seemed as beautiful as it did today.'

Kristin's smile wavered. Somehow, she had begun thinking of Rome as theirs. But that was foolish; she knew Seth had been here before.

'Of course,' she said. 'I forgot this wasn't your first trip.'

He nodded. 'Mmm. I was here twice last year, for Harbrace. And several times before that.'

'On business? Or—or for pleasure?'

'Both. The first time was years ago. I was with——'

'It doesn't matter,' she said quickly.

'Kristin.' Seth lifted her face gently to his. 'The first time I saw Rome, I was fresh out of college, bumming around Europe with two guys from my fraternity.' His eyes met hers. 'I've never been here with a woman, if that's what you're thinking.'

She stared at him, and then she pulled away and buried her face against his shoulder.

'I'm sorry,' she whispered. 'I guess I'm just tired.'

Seth wrapped his arms around her. 'It's late.' He kissed the top of her head. 'Why don't we go to bed?'

His voice was husky. Kristin leaned against him. She could hear the steady beat of his heart beneath her ear.

She knew he wanted to make love to her. But nothing had ever made her feel cheaper than having Vincent leave her after they'd made love. It was the worst possible reminder of just how transitory their relationship had been.

'We have a long day ahead of us tomorrow, Seth. And I'm tired. I need a night's rest.'

'I don't want to leave you, Kristin.' His mouth brushed hers lightly. 'We don't have to make love, if you're too tired. I just want to hold you in my arms while you sleep and awaken with your head on my shoulder.'

What he'd said surprised her. She looked into his eyes, wanting to tell him that she'd had this conversation before, a long time ago—except she had been the one who'd asked her lover to stay, and he'd been the one who'd refused.

'People will find out about us,' he'd said. At the end, she'd understood that was the last thing Vincent had wanted. A relationship that had no future could not be acknowledged in the present.

But how could she explain all that to Seth now? And why should she have to? If Seth really loved her...

'Kristin? What are you thinking?'

She opened her mouth and Vincent's words slipped off her tongue.

'If we spend the night together, people will know about us.'

Seth smiled. 'Who? Signora Giuliano and her little dog?' He laughed. 'I don't think she'll care.'

'What if word somehow gets back to the office?' she said, watching him. 'Won't that bother you?'

His smile faded. 'Yes,' he said after a moment, 'I suppose it would.'

There was a sudden hollow feeling deep within her breast. 'Well, then,' she said tonelessly.

Seth sighed. 'For a moment there, I forgot what Harbrace is like. The damned rumour mill...' There was a silence. 'Then we'll make this our own little world, darling. Nothing can intrude on it.' He kissed the top of her head, then drew her close. 'We can be lovers here, and be Signor Richards *e* Signorina Marshall at the office.'

She hesitated. Seth was right about the rumour mill. And Harbrace was a conservative company. Who knew how its directors would react to its fast-rising Vice-President taking up with his secretary?

It was all logical. Seth was only trying to protect her.

Then why was the hollow feeling still there?

'I don't know. Maybe—maybe...'

He cursed softly. 'You think too damned much,' he said as he swung her into his arms. 'But I know a way to cure that.'

He strode rapidly through the dark flat to the bedroom. Kristin's heart beat an erratic tattoo as he lowered her slowly to her feet and she felt the hardness of his body against hers.

'Seth,' she whispered, 'wait. Please.'

He kissed her again and again, and after a little while she felt the tension draining from her body.

What he'd promised came true. She stopped thinking. There was nothing but the night and the man in her arms.

But a little bit of the day's joy had vanished.

The next morning, Seth raced up to his flat and dressed, and then they shared a taxi to the office.

'Remember,' he said. 'Just look people straight in the eye and things will be fine.'

His fingers curled around her elbow and he propelled her forward.

'Good morning, Silvana,' he said as they marched past the receptionist.

The woman barely looked up. '*Buon giorno*, Signore Richards, Signorina Marshall.'

It was the same at each desk they passed along the way. No one saw anything strange in the American executive and his American secretary travelling to work together. After all, Harbrace had housed them in the same building—it was only logical. As for the rest, Seth treated her with studied courtesy all through the day. She was Kristin, not Miss Marshall, but then she had been Kristin back in the States, too.

They were, once again, the impersonal employer and his private secretary.

They cabbed home separately—there were some visiting clients from the States, and Seth took them out for drinks.

'I wish you could come with us,' he'd said softly to her as she got ready to leave.

Kristin looked at him. 'But that wouldn't be very discreet, would it?' she asked.

His eyes narrowed. 'No,' he said. 'It wouldn't.'

It had been the only answer possible. She knew that, but it didn't make her feel any better. Alone in her flat, Kristin sighed as she exchanged her suit for jeans and a cotton T-shirt, wondering when—and if—Seth would call.

He didn't call. Instead, there was a knock at her door just after eight, and she opened it to find him standing there, smiling, with an armful of clothing. Before Kristin could say anything, he moved past her.

'It's easier than trotting up and down the stairs all the time,' he said as he made his way to the bedroom. 'I was going to suggest you bring your things up to my place.' He looked at her over his shoulder. 'But I was afraid you'd say "no".'

Kristin leaned against the wall, watching as he put his things away next to hers. Part of her rejoiced in the sight of his elegant suits hanging beside her clothing. But part of her was uneasy.

'Kristin?' He turned to her, his eyes watchful. 'If you really don't want me here, I'll leave.'

When she hesitated, his face darkened. 'All right,' he said, turning back to the wardrobe, 'I'll take my things and——'

'No.' The word was torn from her throat. She hurried across the room and into his open arms. 'No,' she whispered, 'don't. Stay with me, Seth.'

His arms closed around her. Within minutes, they were lost to anything but each other.

After that, they were never apart. Kristin's unease began to fade. It was hard to be anything but happy with Seth. He knew how to make her laugh, how to coax a smile from her when none seemed forthcoming. And when she lay in his arms, their mouths and bodies fused with heated urgency, she knew that there was nowhere else she ever wanted to be.

But there were moments when a shadow seemed to blot out the sun. There was the afternoon they literally bumped into each other in the Harbrace reception area. Seth's hands had closed on her shoulders as he'd steadied her.

'Sorry,' he'd said politely.

'My fault,' Kristin had answered with equal courtesy.

And suddenly she'd found herself wishing he would throw propriety to the winds and instead put his arms around her and announce to all the world that he was in love with her.

One afternoon, they were walking slowly through some ancient ruins. Seth was talking about the Roman Empire, how it had finally collapsed with its treasures turned to dust, when suddenly a tiny voice inside her said slyly, You see? Nothing lasts forever.

Kristin shuddered.

'What is it, darling?' Seth asked, putting his arm around her.

She smiled and made some foolish comment about the tumbled ruins. But it took a long time for the unexpected sense of despair to fade.

She told herself her concerns were foolish. Seth was not Vincent—and this was Italy, not Oklahoma.

Still, she found herself wishing that she'd told Seth about Vincent's betrayal of her trust. The past didn't matter, he'd said, but she wasn't as sure about that as she'd once been.

Maybe it was time to get things out in the open, she thought one evening as she dressed for dinner. Seth still thought she'd lived with a man in New York. Didn't he have the right to know that hadn't been true? She could afford to admit it now, even though it would be embarrassing. After all, she'd only kept silent to protect herself from getting involved with him—and see how successful that had been.

And she had to tell him about her long-ago affair. It would be painful: it still hurt to remember that she'd been so foolish as to have thought herself in love with a man like Vincent. But it was Seth's love that had finally healed that wound. Didn't he deserve to know that, too?

A weight seemed to lift from her shoulders. She would tell Seth everything, she decided. And if he didn't want to talk about his past, that was all right. He could keep his secrets. He was hers now, and that was all that mattered.

Hurriedly, she put on her shoes and grabbed her purse. Seth had stayed late at the office. Kristin was meeting him for dinner at a little trattoria they'd discovered near the Campo dei Fiori. Signora Giuliano had recommended it; it pleased the old woman when they told her they'd begun dining there often.

She paused as she entered the restaurant and searched the room for him.

There he was, sitting at a quiet table in the corner. As always, her heart quickened at the sight of him. She started towards him, and then she stopped.

All of a sudden, telling him about herself didn't seem quite so easy. Would he be angry that she'd let him think she'd had a lover back home? Would he think less of her once he knew she'd made a fool of herself years ago?

'Kristin.'

She blinked. Seth had risen to his feet; he was watching her with a questioning smile on his lips. She ran her tongue over her lips, then forced an answering smile to her face and walked to his table.

'Hello,' she said as she slipped into a chair. 'Am I late?'

He sat down opposite her. 'You're right on time,' he said. 'It just seems like an eternity when I'm without you.'

She smiled nervously. 'That's nice.' She looked at him again, then quickly away. 'Did you order yet?'

Seth shook his head. 'Only a bottle of wine.'

'Well,' she said, 'how was your meeting?'

His brows drew together. 'That Valenti is getting to be a first-class pain. I guess he still hasn't gotten over not getting my job.'

She stared at him. 'Marco wanted your job? But surely he wasn't qualified.'

Seth shrugged. 'Try telling him that. He just looks for chances to...' He paused, then reached across the table for her hand. 'Hey,' he said softly, 'what am I doing?' He smiled. 'Here I am, sitting with the most beautiful woman in Rome...'

'Here you are, sitting with the hungriest woman in Rome,' Kristin said. God! She was so nervous. It was silly to be...

'Kristin?' Seth's hand tightened on hers. 'What is it?'

'Nothing. I just—I...' Their eyes met. Tell him, she thought, and she took a deep breath. 'Seth, do you remember that day at Villa d'Este?'

He smiled. 'How could I forget?' he asked softly.

Kristin ran her tongue over her lips. 'You said—you said, that day, that you didn't believe in playing true confessions.'

Seth's eyes narrowed. 'What I said was that the past didn't matter. And you agreed with me.'

She nodded. 'I—I thought that was so, Seth. But—but the past does matter. You can't just——'

'You can.'

'*I* can't, then.' She drew a steadying breath. 'I've tried, Seth. But I can't forget...'

His hand squeezed hers so hard that she flinched. 'What is it?'

Get it over with, she told herself. 'I'm trying to tell you that—that this isn't working,' she said softly. 'You and I——'

'Signore Richards.'

Kristin caught her breath and her gaze flew to the man who'd suddenly loomed over their table. Seth's face darkened.

'Valenti,' he said flatly. 'What are you doing here?'

Marco's eyes went to the table, where Kristin's hand lay clasped in Seth's.

'I am so happy to see that you and the *signorina* found time to relax and see my beautiful city.'

Seth let go of Kristin's hand, pushed his chair back, and rose to his feet. 'What do you want?' he asked in a hard, cold voice.

Marco reached into his pocket and pulled out an envelope. 'A cable arrived for you just after you left the office. I tried calling your flat, but there was no answer, and, seeing how urgent it was, I thought I'd better deliver it in person.' A slow, insinuating smile curled across his mouth. 'Your charming neighbour was out taking the air. She said you weren't in, and suggested I try this place. She said it had become one of your favourites.'

Seth snatched the envelope from the other man's hand. 'Good evening, Valenti,' he said coldly.

There was a silence, and then Marco bowed. 'Enjoy your dinner,' he said.

Seth let out his breath as soon as they were alone again. 'Well,' he said, 'the cat's out of the bag now.'

'Maybe he won't——'

He laughed coldly. 'He'll have the story around so fast it'll make your head spin.'

Kristin folded her hands tightly in her lap. 'And will that upset you?' she said softly.

He stared at her. 'What do you think?'

She looked away quickly. 'I—I have to go to the ladies' room,' she said, reaching for her bag.

Seth tore open the envelope and began reading the cable.

'Damn it!'

Kristin paused. 'What's the matter? Is it bad news?'

'I have to fly to New York immediately.' He crumpled the cable and tossed it into the ashtray. 'The MacArthur merger's in trouble. The board's called an emergency meeting.'

Kristin sank back into her chair. 'When must you leave?'

He smiled grimly. 'In two hours. Valenti's very efficient,' he said, holding out a note that had been attached to the cable. 'He called the airport and arranged a seat for me.'

'How long will you be gone?'

Seth looked at her. 'Two days, three at the most.' His eyes met hers. 'These last weeks have been wonderful,' he said. 'Will you remember that, Kristin?'

Inexplicably, her eyes filled with tears. 'Yes,' she whispered, and then, before Seth could see what was happening to her, she rose to her feet. 'If you're going to make that plane, you'll have to hurry.'

A few hours later he was in a plane high over the Atlantic, and she was alone.

The next day was Saturday. Kristin spent it in her flat, busying herself with a series of mindless chores. She missed Seth terribly, but she also had a growing sense of unease. Something was wrong; she felt it in her bones.

Sunday dawned grey and rainy, but waking to gloom wasn't as bad as waking without Seth. Her bed was a lonely place, and she escaped it, and the flat, as quickly as she could manage.

She spent the day tramping through the Vatican Museums, gaping at the treasures of the Popes along with a horde of other tourists. But her thoughts were four thousand miles away. What was Seth doing? Was he thinking of her? And the despicable little voice within her added another question. Was he alone?

It felt strange to go to the office without him on Monday. Was it her imagination, or did Silvana give her a knowing look as she passed the reception desk? She felt uncomfortable, and she spent the day in her office, leaving it only for lunch. When she got back, there was a note on her desk. Mr Richards had phoned; he would be arriving on the eight p.m. flight.

She was home by six, and nearly crazy with anticipation by seven. She made herself some tea, then looked at the clock again. The minute hand had hardly moved. How would she ever fill the time?

The answer came quickly. She'd make an elegant little supper to welcome Seth home. He'd probably be hungry anyway; she remembered that he hadn't eaten very much when they'd flown to Rome.

'Airline food always looks better than it tastes,' he'd said with a smile.

She went into the kitchen and poked in the fridge. There was a piece of Bel Paese cheese and another of fresh mozzarella. Tomatoes, too, and some basil. Good. And there was some *prosciutto*, and half a melon from the wonderful market at Campo dei Fiori. Kristin arranged the things on a tray, then took down a bottle of olive oil, a tin of anchovies, and a box of water biscuits.

What else? she thought. Wine. Of course. Seth said it was one of the nicest things about Italy, the fact that a meal wasn't a meal without a good bottle of *vino*.

But all she had was a half bottle of Asti Spumante. It wasn't enough; besides, it had sat too long. All the fizz was probably gone. Well, that was no problem. Seth had wine in his flat, a whole case of it.

'A gigantic walk-in closet, that's what my flat is,' he'd joked one evening when they went up to collect some wine and some additional items of his clothing.

Kristin dug out the spare key and trotted up the stairs. She made her way quietly down the hall and held her breath as she unlocked Seth's door. Signora Giuliano lived just across the corridor. The last thing she wanted to do was let the old woman hear her. There was no time to stand around chatting, not when Seth would be home in less than...

The hair rose on the back of her neck as she stepped into his flat. Were those voices she heard, drifting from the living-room? A woman's voice—and now a man's.

Seth's.

Kristin put her hand to her throat. Seth couldn't be back. He'd have come to see her first, he'd have missed her and wanted her and...

'I can't believe you talked me into dropping everything and flying over here with you, Seth.' The woman laughed softly. 'But then, you always were persuasive when you put your mind to it.'

Kristin swayed. No. It couldn't be. It couldn't.

Seth chuckled. 'Come on, admit it. You're glad you came with me.'

Kristin held her breath as she tiptoed down the hall. She paused at the arched entrance to the living-room. Seth was sitting in an easy chair, facing away from her. The woman was out of sight, but...

The woman laughed, and a chill raced along Kristin's spine. She knew that laugh. She knew that voice—that softly feminine, yet oddly husky voice.

It belonged to Jeanne Lester.

For a few terrible seconds, Kristin feared she was going to faint. The room spun away, and she leaned back against the wall, hugging it and the darkness.

She wanted to run away, to race out the door and down the stairs and pretend this wasn't happening.

Jeanne was still talking, her voice low and intimate. 'I should have come with you from the start,' she said. There was the sound of silk shifting against silk. 'Can you ever forgive me?'

Seth laughed softly. 'Don't I always?'

There was a moment's silence, and then Jeanne yawned. 'Sorry,' she said. 'I guess what I need is a good night's sleep.'

'My bed's waiting,' Seth answered.

Kristin caught her bottom lip between her teeth and bit down on it until the rusty taste of blood filled her mouth.

'Seth? What about Kristin?'

He sighed. 'I don't know,' he said. There was the sound of springs giving, and then male footsteps crossed the floor. 'I'll think of something.'

'Umm. I certainly hope so.' High heels tapped lightly across the floor. 'Have I told you how much I missed you?'

'Me, too.' Seth's voice purred with self-satisfaction. 'And that other thing's all over? You're sure?'

'Charlie?' Jeanne sighed. 'I told you, you were right all along. He wasn't for me.'

'I'm glad to hear you admit it, sweetheart. Now come on, stop fighting the inevitable and let me take you to bed.'

A sob rose in Kristin's throat. She was going to be sick, she thought frantically, she was going to be violently ill.

Seth Richards and Jeanne Lester stepped into the hallway from the living-room, their backs to her, their arms intertwined. Kristin turned away blindly, her hand to her mouth. Swiftly, noiselessly, she retraced her steps. Her feet flew along the marble floor and down the steps. She stumbled into her flat, closed the door behind her, then stood shaking in the darkness.

Hours later, as a 747 carried her swiftly through the sky, she was still trembling.

CHAPTER TWELVE

NEW YORK was at its best in the spring. The city's concrete and glass canyons warmed under probing fingers of sunlight. Pink and white cherry blossoms drifted to the grass in Central Park, lightly perfuming the air. For Manhattanites wearied by winter's chill as much as by the day-to-day skirmishes of urban survival, spring was a time of hope.

For Kristin, it was a time of renewal. Winter was gone, and with it had passed the worst months of her life. On this warm May evening, she sat in the quiet green oasis of Gramercy Park counting the small victories that marked her survival.

Her gaze went past the wrought-iron fence that surrounded the private park to one of the houses facing on it. She had a tiny flat in that building, on the third floor. The rent was exorbitant and the flat wasn't really hers—she was sub-leasing it from its elderly owner. But she had no complaints. This area of the city was new to her, which meant she really felt as if she'd made a fresh start. And her new job paid well enough so that she could afford to carry the rent.

A few months ago, all of that had seemed impossible. The night she'd fled Rome—and Seth—her life was nothing but a collapsed house of cards. Standing in a cold, drizzling rain outside the International Arrivals building at Kennedy Airport, Kristin had looked around her blankly, fighting against the sudden swell of panic rising within her.

Her instincts for survival, not planning, had taken her that far. She knew only that facing Seth again would have destroyed her.

But deciding what to do next seemed beyond her capabilities. Standing in the wet New York night, Kristin felt disconnected from reality—for long moments, she didn't even realise that the rain had turned to snow, that she was shaking with the cold.

Instinct took over again. She hailed a taxi and directed it to a small hotel just off Madison Avenue. She'd never been there, but she remembered that Harbrace sometimes booked out-of-town clients into it. And, with a glibness that surprised her, she talked herself into being granted the reduced corporate rate.

That exhausted her emotional resources. She hung a 'Do Not Disturb' sign on the doorhandle and fell into the bed. When she awoke, it was night again. She turned on the TV and stayed in the room for the next two days, staring at the screen but seeing nothing, wallowing in equal parts of hatred for Seth and pity for herself, subsisting on the little tins of orange and tomato juice which were stocked in the room's tiny refrigerator.

On the third morning, catching a glimpse of herself in the mirror, she was stunned at what she saw. Her eyes were enormous in her pale face, her hair was lank and dishevelled. Her blouse was not only creased and grimy, it hung loosely across her breasts.

Kristin told herself she looked exactly like what she was, a woman who had been hurt beyond endurance.

Tears filled her eyes.

Look what he's done to you, she thought, staring into the glass. What's life going to be like now? How could you have been such a fool, Kristin? He wanted you to love him, he said, and you knew, you *knew* what he meant by that.

He wanted you to go to bed with him. Life just repeats itself, that's what it does, and now you—you . . .

A prickle of something moved, ghostlike, along her skin.

And now, she thought, she was feeling sorry for herself, just the way she had before.

Kristin's chin rose. So what? She was entitled. The woman in the mirror had every right to crawl into a corner and lick her wounds, if she wanted. She turned away and threw herself across the narrow bed.

An hour later, she rose slowly and stared at her reflection again. Seth had taken everything from her. But he couldn't take her self-respect, not unless she let him. If she stayed here and wallowed in self-pity, she'd do exactly that.

And he wasn't worth it.

Kristin squared her shoulders. All she had left was herself. If she drowned in her own sorrow, she would have only herself to blame. And if she was strong enough to survive, she would have only herself to thank.

It wasn't much to build on, but it was a beginning.

She had stared at her reflection until the image began to blur, and then she marched into the bathroom. A brisk hot shower later, dressed as carefully as if she were going to work at Harbrace, she had marched out, determined to face the world.

Now, she shivered and rose slowly to her feet as a sudden breeze blew away the cobwebs of memory. May was a strange month in New York; the weather could change within hours, going from warm to cold with no warning. It was time to call it quits anyway, she thought as she closed the park gate behind her. Tomorrow was a work day, and it would be an even longer one than usual. Hale Stevens wanted her at the office an hour early.

That meant getting up at six instead of seven. Kristin sighed as she climbed the steps to her flat. Stevens was almost three times her age. If he could manage, so could she. Besides, he'd warned her about how hard she'd work, right from the start.

She'd answered his rather cryptic ad in the *Times* after three days of job-hunting.

'Good pay, bad hours, interesting work,' the ad had read, with nothing else except a box number.

Kristin had written a short letter expressing her curiosity, and a week later she'd found herself in Hale Stevens' townhouse. The old man had interviewed her briefly, interrupting her recitation of her duties at Harbrace with abrupt questions before she could even mention the name of the man she'd worked for.

'Why did you leave Harbrace, Miss Marshall?'

She had barely hesitated. 'For personal reasons, Mr Stevens.'

His cold grey eyes had focused on her face. 'I've been told I'm a hard man to work for,' he'd said. 'I often work ten and twelve hour days, even an occasional Saturday or Sunday. How would you feel about that?'

How else will I fill my life? she'd thought. She'd met Stevens' forthright look with one of her own.

'That depends on what my salary will be, sir,' she'd said politely.

He had permitted himself a smile. 'What did you earn at Harbrace, Miss Marshall?' She'd told him and he'd nodded. 'How does half that again to start sound?' he'd asked.

Kristin had smiled in return. 'It sounds as if you have yourself a secretary.'

She sighed as she unlocked the door to her flat and stepped inside. The job had proven a turning-point. Stevens was a philanthropist who spent his time using his money, and the money he could wheedle out of others, to bring cultural events to the underprivileged parts of the city. He was a cold, uncommunicative man to work for—but that was OK with her. She'd had more than her fill of personal relationships at work, enough to last a lifetime.

The job proved to be perfect. The time flew by during the day, and she never voiced any complaint about working extra hours.

Kristin double-locked the front door, then switched on the lights. In fact, everything had been going just fine—until a few weeks ago. Suddenly, for no reason at all, she had begun dreaming again.

The dreams were, as they had been months before, about Seth. But now there was an intensity to them that left her trembling. She dreamed of being in his arms, the feel of his kisses so real she would awaken half expecting to find her lips warm and bruised by his.

That she should dream about Seth stunned her. Why was it happening? It made no sense. She'd reached the point where she didn't think about him—not often, anyway, and never with anything approximating kindness.

Kristin kicked off her shoes and padded into the kitchen. It was upsetting. And humiliating. Lately, she'd found herself thinking it might help if she could talk to someone. But there wasn't anyone she was close enough to—and then, just last weekend, she had literally bumped into Susan on Fifth Avenue.

'Excuse me,' they'd both muttered, and then they'd stared, burst into delighted laughter, and grabbed each other in tight hugs.

'My God, look who's here,' Susan had squealed. 'What are you doing in New York? Aren't you still supposed to be in Rome? Why haven't you called me?'

Kristin had smiled. 'It's the same old Susan,' she'd said. 'Ten questions at once and no time to answer one of them.'

Susan had grinned. 'Come on,' she'd said, taking Kristin's arm, 'let's go have lunch and you can tell me everything.'

At first, seeing Susan had been lovely. They'd spent long minutes catching up.

'I'm an experienced world traveller,' Susan had said, waggling her eyebrows. 'I fly all ze time to Paree, *ma petite*.' She'd giggled and reached for a breadstick. 'Terrific, no?'

'Terrific, yes,' Kristin had said with a smile. 'I'm impressed.'

'So? Tell me about yourself. When did you get back from Italy?'

Kristin had felt her smile slipping. 'Months ago,' she'd said offhandedly.

Susan had made a face. 'And you haven't called me? For shame.'

'Well, I've been awfully busy, Suze. I had to find an apartment, and a job.'

'A job? Don't tell me you finally got tired of working for the slave-driver!'

Kristin had nodded. 'Yes,' she said with casual ease, 'I found something much better.' And she'd gone on to explain that she was private secretary to Hale Stevens.

Susan had grinned. 'The old guy who gives away all the money? I hope his philanthropy extends to your salary.'

They'd both laughed, and then they'd chatted for a while longer until Susan had begun to frown. After a few minutes, she'd suddenly cut into Kristin's description of her new flat.

'Why am I getting negative vibes?' she'd said softly.

'What are you talking about, Suze?'

'You tell me,' Susan had said warily. 'You've got shadows under your eyes. And you've lost weight.'

'A few pounds off never hurts,' Kristin had said, trying to make light of what she knew was the truth. That was what came of not sleeping well—but she couldn't tell that to Susan.

Or could she? Susan was her friend; she'd understand. Tell her, Kristin had thought and, for one wild moment, she almost had.

But what could she tell her? The whole ugly story about Seth and their affair? That was bad enough, but what would Susan think if she told her that lately the man she hated had invaded her dreams?

It was hard enough to face that herself.

Somehow, she'd managed to smile and assure Susan that she was fine, just a little tired from the pressures of her new job, and then she'd looked at her watch, pleaded an appointment, and hurried off.

'Call me,' Susan had yelled after her, and she'd promised she would.

But she hadn't. And she wouldn't. Not until these damned dreams stopped.

Kristin sighed and switched off the kitchen light. She was too tired to think any more. It had been an exhausting day. Stevens had dictated letters all morning, and she'd spent half the afternoon on the telephone with the members of a committee he'd formed to raise funds to bring over a Russian ballet troupe.

A frown creased her forehead as she opened the bedroom window. And then there'd been that nonsense at the end of the day. She'd been tallying up some figures when she'd looked up to see a tall, dark-haired man in the doorway.

For one pulse-stopping moment, Kristin had imagined it was Seth. Her heart had done a skittish little dance, and she'd half risen to her feet before she realised it wasn't.

Flustered, Kristin had given the stranger a quick smile. 'I thought—I thought you were someone I knew,' she'd said.

The man had smiled back. 'I'm sorry I'm not,' he'd said, 'considering the way you looked when you saw me.'

'Well, he took you by surprise,' she said to the mirror as she reached for her pyjamas, her voice strong and deliberate in the silent bedroom. 'If Fate ever really does you the kindness of propelling Seth Richards through the door, you'll do what you should have done that night in Rome. You'll walk right up to him and slap his face hard enough to make his ears ring.'

She finished the thought with a nod of determination, then pulled on her pyjamas. She'd given up nightgowns and things made of silk; they had no place in her new life.

Yawning, Kristin got into bed and shut off the lamp, plunging the room into darkness. Lord, she was bone-weary. A night without dreams would be wonderful. Please, she thought, let this be that night. Let this be...

Her lashes fluttered drowsily. After a few minutes, Kristin slept.

She slept dreamlessly through the soft May night while the moon rose over the city, then fell gently in the sky. Just after dawn a breeze drifted through the open window, a warm breeze that feathered a light caress along her skin.

She stirred under its touch and sighed a man's name into the early morning stillness. The breeze moved across her again, as fresh and gentle as a lover's breath. Kristin stirred. And slowly, with deft delicate brushstrokes, her subconscious mind began to paint a scene.

She was standing in a high tower, gazing out on to a vista far below. Cliffs rose up from the valley floor, where the shadows lay deepest. Beyond, boats rode a distant waterway. A golden disc hung in a sky so blue it brought a catch to her throat.

Suddenly, there was a sound behind her. The hair rose on hr nape; an awareness quickened her blood.

'Kristin.'

Her heart stumbled, then began to race.

'Kristin.'

She turned and there he was, standing in the doorway, smiling.

'Seth,' she said, and suddenly she was flying across the room to him.

His arms opened and gathered her in. 'My love,' he whispered.

Kristin lifted her face for his kiss. Tears rose in her eyes. It had been so long. So long...

The shrill cry of the telephone catapulted her upright. Disorientated, Kristin clutched the blankets to her breasts. Her pyjamas were damp with sweat, and she shivered as the soft breeze chilled the room.

The phone rang again, and she reached out and snatched it up.

'Hello?'

'Good morning, Miss Marshall.'

Kristin blinked. 'Mr Stevens?' The bedside clock read five fifty-five a.m. 'Is something wrong?'

The old man's voice wheezed through the line. 'I'm afraid I'll have to change our plans for this morning.'

Kristin sank back against the pillows. 'I see,' she said calmly, as if six a.m. wake-up calls were an everyday occurrence.

'United Investment's agreed to consider backing the Russians. I've a breakfast tête-a-tête with their new CEO, and then a ten a.m. meeting with his board of directors. I should like you to bring my notes to the United boardroom a few minutes before that.'

Kristin sighed. 'Of course, Mr Stevens.'

The quavering voice sharpened. 'Please be prompt, Miss Marshall.'

Kristin shook her head as she swung her legs to the floor. As if she were ever anything but.

'Certainly,' she said. 'I'll see you then.'

She hung up the phone and put her hands to her temples and pushed back her heavy fall of dark hair.

Stevens had made a simple enough request. Why, then, did she suddenly feel so uneasy?

At a quarter to ten, Kristin stepped out of the lift and smiled at the young woman seated at the reception desk before her. She was on the executive level of United Investment; the company occupied the top ten floors of a glass and steel high rise building near the South Street Seaport, not far from the Harbrace offices. Kristin had not been in the area for months. She hadn't avoided it—there was little likelihood of running into Seth or any of her old co-workers. But being in this neighbourhood only added to the unease that had been with her ever since Hale Stevens' early morning phone call.

'Miss Marshall?' The girl at the reception desk smiled pleasantly. 'Welcome to the United Tower.'

Kristin's smile dimmed. 'The what?'

'The Tower. That's what we call it.' She smiled again. 'You're early. The boardroom's just down that corridor, but nobody's there yet.'

'That's fine. I'll just leave some papers for Mr Stevens and be on my way.'

The sooner, the better, she thought as she walked towards the boardroom. Her disquietude was growing stronger by the second.

She paused in the open doorway, taking in the room's enormous size. Harbrace had a luxurious boardroom, but it paled compared to this. Carpeting, as deep as spring grass, stretched ahead to a wall of smoky glass. An enormous burled walnut table dominated the room. Chairs were drawn up around it, awaiting the board members. Each place was set with a crystal water goblet and matching carafe, notepaper, and pencils.

Kristin's gaze went back to the wall of glass at the far end of the room. Slowly, as if drawn by an invisible hand, she walked towards it.

She stopped just short of the window, overcome by a sudden surge of vertigo. But that was impossible; she didn't have a problem with heights. The view from Seth's office at Harbrace had been much like this, and it had never bothered her.

She took a hesitant step forward and looked out. The city stretched far below, the narrow canyons of the financial district dappled with shade where the bright sun had yet to reach. The river lay beyond; tug boats moved slowly along the sluggish grey waters like children's toys in a stream. High above, in a sky so blue it looked as if it had been painted on, the sun hung like a giant gold disc.

It was like standing in a tower and looking out over a kingdom. It was like...

Kristin's heart skittered wildly. Get out, the voice inside her whispered, go on, get out now.

But it was too late. She knew it even before she turned towards the doorway and...

Hale Stevens was standing just inside it, watching her. It was all she could do not to laugh with relief.

So much for dreams, she thought, and she smiled politely.

'Good morning, sir.'

Stevens nodded and started towards her. There was a sea of faces behind him. The members of United's board of directors nodded pleasantly as they filed into the room and gathered around the conference table.

Her employer took the briefcase she handed him. 'Did Ivanovitch phone about the proposed tour dates?'

She nodded. 'Yes. I thought you might want the memo, so I brought it. I have it right...'

Oh God. Kristin felt as if the floor were tilting. Far across the room, a man stepped briskly through the doorway. He was tall, broad-shouldered, with glossy dark hair. The other men in the room turned towards him deferentially, their body language eloquently proclaiming him their leader.

Her heart hammered wildly against her ribs.

It was Seth.

Kristin spun away and stared blindly out of the window. Where was all that brave rhetoric about what she'd do if ever she saw Seth Richards again? All she wanted was to run, to hide in some dark corner.

'...and take notes, please, Miss Marshall.'

Stevens was talking to her. Somehow, she managed to turn towards him.

'I—I'm sorry,' she said. 'What were you saying, Mr Stevens?'

'I said I'd like you to stay and take notes, Miss Marshall.'

Her eyes flew to Seth again. He was at the head of the conference table now. In another few minutes he'd see her. He...

His head lifted slowly. Kristin's heart stopped beating. She shrank back, but there was nowhere to run. The window was behind her, and ahead—and ahead...

Seth's eyes fixed on her. She stared at him, watching as the colour drained from his face. The man beside him was saying something to him; she saw him nod, but she knew that he hadn't heard what the man was saying, any more than she could hear Hale Stevens.

Her first thought was that he hadn't changed at all. But then, why would he? Months had passed since she'd seen him; not the years her lonely, angry heart claimed.

But he had changed. The signs were subtle, but they were there. There were grooves beside his mouth, and the laugh lines that fanned out from his eyes seemed more pronounced. Strands of silver streaked the dark hair that grew back from his temples.

His face hardened, and she saw the sudden flash of contempt in his eyes before he looked away from her.

'Gentlemen,' he said. 'Please, be seated.'

Hale Stevens' bony hand closed on Kristin's elbow. 'Where are you going?' he muttered.

She stared at him. 'I—I'm leaving. I...'

'Whatever is wrong with you today, young woman?' The old man propelled her to a chair in the corner. 'I want notes, I said.'

'But——'

'Miss Marshall.' Seth's cold voice filled the room. Every eye turned towards her.

'Does Richards know you?' Stevens whispered.

Kristin nodded unhappily. 'I—I worked for him. I——'

'Miss Marshall.' Seth smiled unpleasantly. 'This Board has important business to conduct. Kindly take your seat and let it do so.'

Colour raced into her cheeks. She saw the raised eyebrows, the surprised looks, and she sat quickly and took a notepad and pencil from her shoulder-bag.

The next hour was like a nightmare. Kristin scribbled furiously into her notepad, but she had no idea what she was writing. She heard Seth's voice, the voice of others, but not what they were saying. Finally, she heard the scrape of chairs and she looked up.

Men were rising to their feet. The meeting was over.

Kristin rose, too. The board members were streaming from the room, Hale Stevens among them, deep in conversation with the man next to him. And Seth—her breath caught. Seth was standing at the head of the table, watching her, and she suddenly knew how a sheep felt when it met the cold, inscrutable gaze of the wolf.

Quickly, she gathered her things together and started towards the door.

'Mr Stevens,' she called, 'wait.'

'Close the door after you, Weems.'

The last man in the straggling line looked back. His eyes went from Seth to Kristin. But Seth's words had been a command, not a request. The man nodded, and before Kristin could reach it, the door swung shut.

The room filled with a silence so profound she could hear the sound of it beating like ocean waves against the window-panes. Kristin kept her eyes straight ahead, on the closed door, and finally she began walking steadily towards it.

She almost made it. She was halfway there when Seth stepped towards her and caught her by the shoulder.

'Where in hell do you think you're going?'

Be calm, Kristin told herself.

'Let go of me,' she said quietly.

Seth's fingers bit into her flesh. 'I asked you a question.'

Her heart skittered wildly. 'Let go of me, I said.'

'So you can run?' He laughed. 'No, Kristin. Not this time.'

'Damn you, Seth!' Her voice rose. 'You have no right to—— '

She gasped as his grip on her tightened. 'Look at me,' he said. Slowly, she did as he'd ordered. His eyes were glacial, the pupils dark. 'We can do this the easy way or the hard way, Kristin. You can either sit down, or——'

Kristin's chin rose. 'I don't have to take orders from you, Seth. I don't work for you any——'

He uttered a short, crude word and caught hold of her wrist. 'Don't push me,' he said. His mouth twisted. 'And believe me, it won't take much.'

Her eyes met his. 'That's it,' she said quietly. 'If you can't get what you want by asking, try bullying. It worked before.'

The cold mask slipped from his face for an instant. 'I never bullied you, Kristin,' he said softly. 'Whatever happened between us happened because it was what we both wanted.'

Kristin felt as if a hand had closed around her heart. 'Seth, please, let me leave. There's no point in——'

His eyes frosted over. 'No. Not this time. I know that running away is your speciality, but I'll be damned if I'll help you do it.' He smiled grimly. 'I'll let you go, all right—but first I want some answers.'

'Well,' she said, 'there we are. The old Seth is back.' She tossed her head and looked up at him. 'What Seth wants, Seth gets. And the hell with—with . . .'

Her voice broke. She twisted free of his grasp and walked quickly to the window, despising herself for the sudden catch in her throat.

Seth cursed again, then snatched at the telephone. 'Lillie? Hold my calls. Yes, all of them.' The phone slammed down, and suddenly he was behind Kristin, his hands on her shoulders as he spun her towards him. 'All right,' he said fiercely, 'all right, let's have it.'

Kristin swallowed hard. 'Have what? I don't know what——'

His eyes glared into hers. 'Why did you run away from me?'

'I didn't run,' she said. 'I left.'

'Yeah. In the middle of the night, without leaving so much as a note or a message or a forwarding address.'

Kristin twisted free of him. 'What's the matter?' she said bitterly. 'Did I spoil your plans?'

Seth's eyes glittered dangerously. 'Yes,' he said softly, 'you might say that.'

'I know you've had a lot of practice saying goodbye, Seth. But if you're waiting for me to apologise for denying you the pleasure——'

'Ah,' he said coldly, 'I see. You couldn't handle a goodbye scene. That's why you ran out on me in the middle of the——'

'You're right,' Kristin said sharply, 'I couldn't handle it. Once you've survived one, you don't much feel like living through another.'

'I knew you were going back to him,' he said bitterly. 'I knew it before I left for New York. I just never dreamed you'd——'

Kristin stared at him. 'What are you talking about?'

'You and he had no commitment, you said. Hell, I almost believed you. But you always held something back, and I knew what it was. I didn't want to, but I knew. You never stopped loving that bastard...'

'What?'

Seth's hands closed on her shoulders. 'Did he welcome you with open arms, Kristin?' His eyes grew dark. 'Did he still want you, even though you'd just come warm from my bed?'

She stared at him blankly. Seth thought—he thought she'd left him for her lover. Her supposed lover. Her imaginary...

Hysterical laughter rose in her throat. She'd dented Seth Richards' ego by leaving him before he could leave her. Well, she could heap insult on injury. And, by God, she would!

'I'm sure he would have wanted me,' she said. Her eyes met his. 'That is, he would have—if he'd ever existed.'

Seth's hands bit into her. 'What the hell are you talking about?'

The stunned look on his face gave her a bitter-sweet pleasure.

'Prepare yourself for a shock, Mr Richards. I didn't leave you for another man. There *was* no other man.'

His face whitened. 'Don't lie to me, Kristin. Your lover——'

'You're the one who decided I had a lover,' she said. 'All I said was that I had a room-mate. And I did—a girl named Susan.'

He stared at her, then drew a ragged breath. 'Then why did you let me think...?'

Kristin's mouth trembled. 'I don't know. No. That's not true. I—I thought you were beginning to—to be interested in me.'

He laughed, the sound harsh as sandpaper. 'That's one way to put it.'

'And I thought—I thought it would give me some protection if you thought—if you believed...' She touched the tip of her tongue to her lips. 'Look, it doesn't much matter now, does it? You wanted to end our affair. Well, it ended. Isn't that what counts?'

'Our affair?' Seth's voice was dangerously quiet. 'Yes, I guess that's all it was to you, Kristin. It was fun, for a while, but then you wanted out. And——'

'I wanted out?' Her chin rose in defiance. 'At least have the decency to be honest about it,' she said. 'Vincent was a lot of things, but at least he—he didn't lie. He...'

Her voice broke and she swung away from him and buried her face in her hands.

'Vincent?' Seth's voice was harsh. 'Who the hell is Vincent?'

The truth was all coming out at last, Kristin thought wearily. But what good could it possibly do now?

'A man I worked for years ago. I thought—I thought I was in love with him, and that he loved me. So I—I let myself get involved with him, and then he—he walked away, the same as—as...'

'Kristin. Look at me.'

His hands closed lightly on her shoulders. 'No,' she whispered brokenly.

'Please, Kristin.'

She turned slowly towards him, her eyes glittering with unshed tears. Her courage was failing her. Months of anger and rage had left her emotions too near the surface.

'Seth,' she whispered, 'I can't go through this. I—I haven't the heart for it.'

'Kristin.' He looked into her eyes. 'Why did you leave me?'

'You were going to leave me, Seth. I just—I just made the first move.'

'Leave you?' he said. 'Leave you? After I'd flown back to New York and put my job on the line? After I'd faced the board of directors and said, listen, you old bastards, Valenti's going to spread rumours about the woman I love, and——'

Kristin's head came up. 'About who?'

He smiled. 'About you. Who else would I mean?'

She shook her head. A tiny flame of hope flared to life within her, and then died.

'That's a lie. You brought Jeanne Lester back to Rome with you. I saw her. I heard...'

Seth groaned softly. 'Kristin, my love. My darling. It's all beginning to make sense. You thought Jeanne and I——'

'"My bed's waiting," you said.' Angry tears rose in her eyes and she brushed them away with the back of her hand. 'I heard every word, Seth. You can't lie your way out of it. You went to New York for a board meeting, and while you were there, Jeanne Lester——'

Seth caught her wrists. 'And while I was there,' he said gently, 'the Harbrace Board offered me the top spot at the company they'd just acquired.'

'United Investment is—is MacArthur?'

He nodded. 'I told them I'd accept the job—if they'd accept my news. I said I'd fallen in love with the best damned secretary any man had ever had, that I was going to marry her when I could find a way to convince her that marrying me was——'

Kristin's mouth dropped open. 'You're making this up,' she whispered.

Seth smiled. 'I love you,' he said.

'But—but Jeanne...'

'Jeanne is my half-sister.'

Kristin swayed. 'Your half-sister?'

'Yes. She says I'm overly protective—well, maybe I am. But I only want what's best for her. She'd only been in New York a short while before I had to take the Rome assignment, but it had been long enough for her to fall for some jerk. I thought she'd give him up for the chance to go to Italy with me, but I couldn't talk her into it.'

'Oh, Seth. I thought—I thought . . .'

His arms closed around her. 'I was worried sick about Jeannie in the weeks before I left New York. I almost told you about her half a dozen times.' A muscle knotted in his jaw. 'But how could I complain to you about the foolishness of my kid sister getting involved with some guy who wasn't good enough for her when I thought you were carrying a torch for the same kind of bastard?'

Kristin looked at him. 'You never said you loved me until this minute.'

Seth shook his head. 'Didn't I? No, I suppose I didn't. You thought I was the world's worst philanderer, sweetheart. So I avoided doing or saying anything that might smack of that. I wanted to make everything new and special.' He clasped her shoulders tightly. 'I love you and I want to share my life with you, Kristin. And I've never said that to any woman before.'

'Oh, Seth.' Kristin took his face in her hands and raised herself to him. 'Seth, I love you. I love you so much.'

He gathered her to him and kissed her, gently at first, the taste of his mouth and the taste of her tears blending, and then his arms tightened and his kiss became fierce and filled with the anguish of the empty months they'd spent apart. When at last Seth raised his head, Kristin was almost dizzy with joy.

The door swung open suddenly. 'There you are,' a familiar, huskily feminine voice said. 'The dragon lady at the reception desk wouldn't let me——' Jeanne Lester halted abruptly. 'Kristin?' she said incredulously.

Seth's arm slipped around Kristin's shoulders. 'I know it's a little late for a formal introduction, but I think you ladies deserve one. Kristin, this is my half-sister, Jeanne.' He smiled. 'And this, Jeannie,' he said, bringing Kristin closely into the protective curve of his arm, 'is Kristin Marshall—the woman I'm going to marry.'

A happy smile spread across Jeanne's face. 'He found you,' she said, relief evident in her voice. 'Thank goodness. The man's been such an ill-tempered bear these past months.'

A young man stepped into the room and put his arm lightly around Jeanne's waist.

'Did you tell your brother the news?' he said.

Jeanne raised her eyebrows. 'Not yet, George,' she said mildly.

Seth's brows rose. 'What news?'

George stepped forward. 'Jeanne has agreed to do me the honour of becoming my wife, sir.'

Jeanne rolled her eyes dramatically. 'Such formality, George,' she said with a touch of impatience. 'George proposed,' she said to Seth. 'And I decided, what the heck, I might as well go for it.'

Seth began to chuckle. 'As you can see,' he said to Kristin, 'my sister and I don't share all the same genes. She has none of my flair for the romantic.'

They smiled at each other. Seth tilted Kristin's face to his and kissed her.

Jeanne cleared her throat. 'OK, big brother,' she said, 'we've got to be going. George just wanted to stop by and let you in on the good news.'

Seth nodded. 'Congratulations,' he said. But his eyes were fixed on Kristin.

The door closed softly, and Kristin and Seth were alone.

'How do you feel about long engagements?' he asked softly.

'Terrible,' Kristin sighed. 'And you?'

'I think anything more than a week is an absolute waste of time.' He kissed her. 'On second thought, a week's too long. If we got the licence this morning...'

She tilted her head back and looked at him. 'Can we do that?'

He smiled. 'Why not? Anything's possible, now that I've got you back. The licence this morning, the wedding this afternoon, and an evening flight to Rome, for our honeymoon. How's that sound?'

'Wonderful,' she whispered.

They smiled at each other, and then Seth drew Kristin to him and kissed her, just as the beams of the sun reached the tower and bathed them both in dazzling gold.

* * * * *

Seth's sister Jeanne has her own story in LOST IN A DREAM, out next month. Watch for it!

Janet Dailey
Americana

Janet Dailey's perennially popular Americana series
continues with more exciting states!

Don't miss this romantic tour of America through
fifty favorite Harlequin Presents novels, each one set
in a different state, and researched by Janet and her
husband, Bill.

A journey of a lifetime in one cherished collection.

April titles   **#29 NEW HAMPSHIRE**
              Heart of Stone

              #30 NEW JERSEY
              One of the Boys

Following the success of WITH THIS RING,
Harlequin cordially invites you to enjoy the
romance of the wedding season with

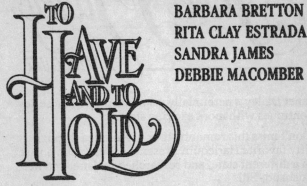

BARBARA BRETTON
RITA CLAY ESTRADA
SANDRA JAMES
DEBBIE MACOMBER

A collection of romantic stories that celebrate the joy,
excitement, and mishaps of planning that special day
by these four award-winning Harlequin authors.

**Available in April at your favorite Harlequin
retail outlets.**

HARLEQUIN *Temptation*

Rebels & Rogues

Jackson: Honesty was his policy...
and the price he demanded of the woman
he loved.

THE LAST HONEST MAN
by Leandra Logan
Temptation #393, May 1992

All men are not created equal. Some are
rough around the edges. Tough-minded but
tenderhearted. Incredibly sexy. The tempting
fulfillment of every woman's fantasy.

When it's time to fight for what they believe in,
to win that special woman, our Rebels and Rogues
are heroes at heart. Twelve Rebels and Rogues,
one each month in 1992, only from
Harlequin Temptation!
